This issue is the cool downdraft that precedes fall. We have seen the towering thunderheads, the churning updrafts that come before the fire, and the dismal quiet that can suffocate us with stillness. Throughout—in spite of it all, perhaps—there are still stories to be heard: stories about seekers, stories about those who are adrift, and stories about how we find our way in unfamiliar landscapes.

This issue is the third instance of the third year, and even though the numbering says otherwise, we know the significance . . .

Underland Arcana is published on a seasonal basis. This issue is published in conjunction with the fall equinox, when snakes and rabbits duck into their wardrobes for different coats.

EDITOR
Mark Teppo

COVER IMAGE
paseven / stock.adobe.com

SIGIL ART
Andrew Penn Romine

PUBLISHER
Underland Press
Clackamas, OR, USA

At noon, even the shadows are parched . . .

UNDERLAND ARCANA

~ 11 ~

Underland Press

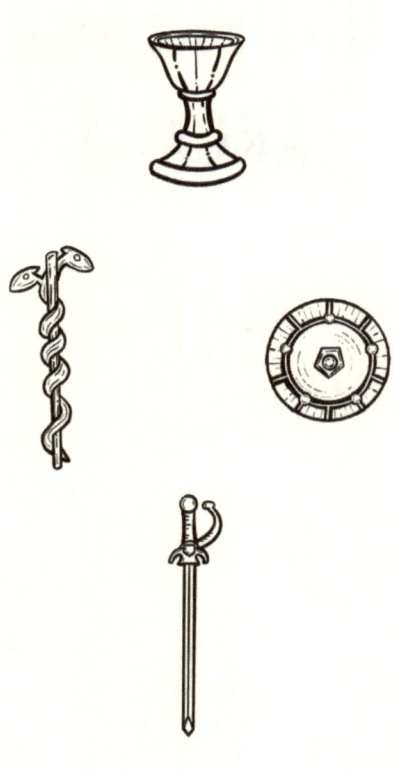

Contents

The Threshold of Possibility

Recently, I found myself with a half hour of time before the next thing happened, and I took advantage of those thirty minutes to get a haircut. I went to a place that wasn't my usual spot, and I sat in the chair of a stylist I didn't know. Which meant we had that small talk dance. "How's your month been?" she asked.

I thought: *Two weeks ago, I went to Fresno, CA, to pack up the final belongings of my recently deceased uncle.* And I decided that was a little personal for first-time sharing. Then, I thought: *Last week, I drove through a street shoot-out and my passenger got hit in the eye with a stray bullet.* And no one is really ready for that to be dropped into casual conversation. And so I said: "It's been an interesting month."

And we moved on to talking about sports and movies and what-not. The Universe remained undisturbed.

It's been a month since the shooting as I write this. It'll be two months when this issue comes out. My friend has been through a transformative event—it's terrible, yes, and tragic—but she has found peace and understanding and wisdom already. Not for the part where our world allows a long and complicated series of circumstances and choices and what-not that create an event that has such an impact on an innocent. That's definitely broken, and yes, there is a lot of rage and frustration there. But for herself, and who she is now—and who she is becoming—that part. Yes, that part has been embraced.

I stand amazed. I stand inspired. I marvel at our ability to use story to find a way through adversity, pain, and setbacks. I like stories that contain a little hope—some ember that can yet be blown into a full flame. And the Arcana is filled with stories that aren't as bleak as they may initially appear, and it will continue to be a conflagration waiting to be born.

And so, as we finish this third year of tickling the edge of uncertainty—as we stand poised to leap again into the unknown—I want to take a moment to remind us that we are stronger than we know. That we are surrounded and supported by those who believe in us. That life is capricious and random, and that love and compassion are infinite. That—no matter what—we get to write our stories in any way we choose.

Mark Teppo
August 15th, 2023

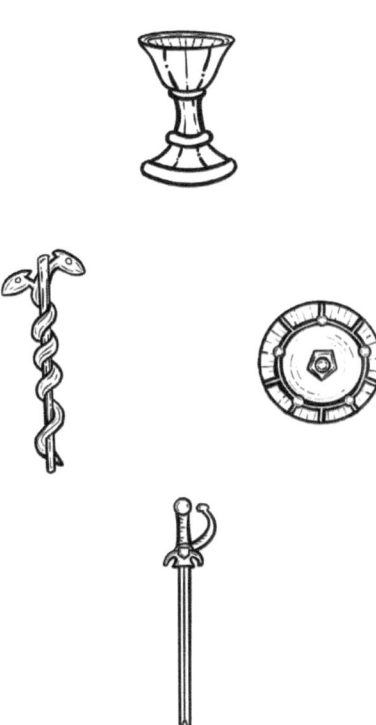

The Raconteur

~ *Phillip E. Dixon*

The crowd's thrilled buzzing filled the stuffy, dimly lit tent. An elongated bulb hovered over a canvas-covered mass on the slat-board stage. The dull, orange filament reminded Jacques of a campfire. He elbowed his skinny thirteen-year-old frame to the front, eager to see the Raconteur. The traveling carnival was incredible, with diving horses, a fight club tent, the punch-a-bag game, and the chicken-eating geeks at the freakshow. He'd seen a real automobile too—a Ford. Best of all, Jacques's lone nickel stayed in his pocket—the carnival was free. And those sweet summer strawberries were too if no one was looking.

"Gather 'round! Gather 'round!"

The Raconteur's voice—the squeaky sound of a ten-year-old boy—carried effortlessly from the stage. Spindly arms gesticulated, setting purple sleeves asway. Eight feet tall, the Raconteur's rainbow-colored cloak enveloped a barrel-shaped body. "Who would like to hear a story—"

The audience hollered.

"Who wants jaded heroes and mysterious villains? Absurd comedy and epic tragedy? Blood and redemption? Love and suspense?"

Jacques's fingers found his ears. The crowd grew more intense with each question—as loud as the Magician's tent when he cut the upside-down woman from the audience vertically in half. It was messy—pig slop, surely—but the blue glow throughout was a fascinating trick.

The Raconteur continued from the stage in his child's pitch. "Who would like to sail the Seas of Devilry and shipwreck on the Shore of Dreams? Who will fight the one-eyed beasts in the Forest of Pillars? Who will seek Eternity's Clock and unchain Mother Time?"

"I will!" Jacques shouted, his voice lost in the audience's roar.

The Raconteur still heard him. "You look like a storyteller, my young friend," the Raconteur said, gliding downstage, wooden face drawing close, boyish voice a near-whisper. A hint of pale gray iris pocked two black eyes, one slightly larger than the other. A tiny mouth dashed across a wood-grained face complete with knotted nose, a sharply hooked corner melting into a pocket of black chin-rot. Atop the scalp perched a smear of sienna-colored hair—a dead, fallen maple leaf.

Jacques shivered, wondering why the man had made such a strange mask.

The Raconteur placed a frigid, twiggy finger under Jacques's chin. "It's in your veins, isn't it?" he asked as if sharing a secret. "A boy far from home, hopping trains, eating bull toads, telling tall tales to whomever will listen. Daydreams of jungles and gunfights—a quicksilver escape from the family dust farm."

Yes.

"A boy in need of an audience."

Yes!

The crowd grew restless.

"Get on with it!"

"Tell us a story!"

The Raconteur's head snapped up. "But a story needs inspiration!" he called. "And where shall we find it?"

"Where?" a man shouted, laughing.

The Raconteur floated back to the stage beside the hidden object. "Why, here among you! You, the people, shall become—" The tarpaulin fell. "The Great Orator!"

Audience members gasped. A metal pig's face of rusted wrought iron overlooked the audience. A blotchy canvas ear drooped on either side, worn leather straps dangling from a missing mouth, eyes empty. It was as tall as the Raconteur. Jacques thought the snout made it look like the gas mask his father had brought home from the war in Somme. Acrid metallic tang filled the air.

The audience began to laugh—some with mirth or drink, some with nerves.

The Raconteur ran his hand over the pig's flat nose, looping around the nostrils. "Every story needs turmoil and passion, wisdom and loss. And, most importantly, we need characters! Who shall play the prankster?"

A hand shot up from the crowd.

"The prankster has been found! And who shall be the gargoyle?"

"My wife!" a man shouted to laughter.

The Raconteur pulled people as they volunteered, sliding through the crowd who instinctively gave him wide berth, his long shadow an eclipse.

"We need a bastard! Are there any bastards among you?"

Cheers erupted, jeers and jostling accompanying a slew of raised arms including Jacques's. Mama had called him one enough times. But the Raconteur passed him without a glance, choosing a barefoot man instead. Jacques let his arm flop, disappointed.

"And the widow?"

"Me!" a little girl in a patched wool skirt shouted. The crowd laughed again. The girl's mother, in a similarly worn skirt, shushed her.

"*Tsk, tsk, tsk.* A mother should encourage her little Alice to tell stories." The Raconteur stroked the girl's hair. "Indeed, a mother should lead by example."

The woman tried to step back, but the people behind stood firm. The Raconteur gripped her arm and dragged her to the stage where she stood, eyes wide and anxious. "We have our widow!"

The little girl started to cry. Jacques sidled over and put his arm around her like one of his little sisters. "Your mama will be fine," he said. "She's gonna tell us a story."

The Raconteur pointed to the volunteers who looked jaundiced beneath the lightbulb. "Four characters shape tonight's tale. They make our treatise." The Raconteur positioned them around and inside the pig's head. He slipped the leather straps around the elderly woman playing the prankster, hoisting her inside the pig, her head becoming its right eye, her grey braid trailing down the pig's cheek like a tear. "Every character has a deep desire—a *need*." The widow took the other eye. The Raconteur helped lay the burly bastard and balding gargoyle down back-to-back, strapping the men's feet to the semi-narrow corners of the pig's upper jaw, then tied their arms and necks together to form the lower jaw. Jacques heard their protests, but the crowd's fever drowned them out.

"A character without motivation is flat, uninteresting, lacking dimension." The Raconteur pointed at Jacques. "Can you suggest a motivation for our characters here?"

"A problem to solve?" Jacques offered, the excitement of recognition tamping his growing unease.

The Raconteur punctuated the air. "That's right, my boy! An obstacle! Our story is almost ready. But *how*—" he hawked the word, "can there be a story if the Great Orator is missing its voice?"

Jacques leapt, eager to be on stage, to act, to be *seen*. The Raconteur pointed at him again but lower, aiming at the widow's little girl. Instinctively, Jacques wanted to shield her, sensing something was awry, but a hairy-armed man beside him hoisted the girl onto the stage. She ran past the Raconteur and wrapped her arms around her mother's strapped-down legs inside the pig's head. The audience laughed.

The Raconteur raised his arms. "The Great Orator, he comes!"

The lightbulb snapped off. Gasps and nervous tittering filled the black tent. Screams from the stage rose alongside crackles and pops like logs in a fire. The crowd froze, a herd of startled rabbits. The screeches rose in pitch and volume. Jacques plugged his ears again, the sound verging on unbearable. Then silence. Blue light filled the pig's eyes and mouth, the lower jaw stretching in a yawn.

The tension broke, and the audience applauded, raucous. The hairy-armed man clapped Jacques on the back and said, "A magic show too!"

In the blue silhouette, Jacques could make out something dripping on stage.

The Grand Orator's mouth moved, and the little girl's voice washed over the rapt crowd. "*Once upon a time . . .*"

The smell of iron grew stronger. Jacques realized the pig's head wasn't covered in rust. He wanted to hear the story, but the voice inside him that warned of Mama's quick hands spoke. *Run.* Jacques hesitated, thinking about the little girl. *Run!* He pushed his way back toward the tent's entrance to slip out.

"Why are you leaving, Jacques? The story has only just begun."

The Raconteur's rainbow cloak blocked the way.

Jacques's voice quavered. "No."

"Ah, but storytelling is a timeless tradition—one which separates man from beast. Story is *life*."

A quiet, hiccupping wail snuck out of Jacques, making him feel like a baby, but he couldn't help it.

"You wanted a story, Jacques. There's a price."

"But—"

"The carnival is free? No. But, you can tell *me* a story.

Nourish me with stories—" The Raconteur opened his cloak "—from the inside."

A naked, withered boy of about ten hung from the Raconteur's fleshless chest, arms threaded through bare ribs piercing his abdomen, legs looping at unnatural angles through the pelvis. The boy's eyes glowed blue.

"*Please,*" the boy said. It was the Raconteur's voice. "No more stories."

Woodpecker

~ *J. Anthony Hartley*

We woke in the house, our house, to silence. I thought it was unusual, then. Every morning, there was the sound of breakfast and the preparations for the day, but not today. My sister met me in the empty kitchen, and we looked at each other in blankness, wondering where they could have gone. After a brief exploration, we found the house was empty. Just us. We hadn't heard them leave. Though we called, there was no response.

Turning on the television did no good. There was nothing but snow, and as I flipped from channel to channel, we looked at each other, wondering and frowning. I shook my head, killed the static hiss, and dropped the remote. Together, we decided to investigate some more. Outside, the car was still in the garage, and all along the street sat empty vehicles. The sky was blue and clear. Along the street lay silence, like a blanket. As we stood there, outside our front door, I reached for her hand in the stillness.

"What are we going to do?" I asked her.

"I don't know," she said, squeezing back.

We stood there absorbing the quiet and wondering. I think then, disbelief swallowed my fear, at least for a while.

Suddenly, the silence was broken by birdsong from the solitary tree in our front yard, and we looked up, together, wondering even more. A small bird emerged from the leaves and took off into the air, flying swiftly across the roofs of empty houses and away and out of sight while we tracked it.

After a while, we went back inside.

The phone gave us nothing but more silence, undercut by a vague and distant hiss, like the far-off sound of waves.

We were too young to know, I guess, to understand. How could we comprehend the power of collective will? You know, there was talk about it on the television, on the internet, in many places, discussions of cults and new religions and the like, but back then, I didn't even understand what a cult was. Eventually, it turned out to be a movement, nothing else, but even that was enough. They couldn't know either, what power they had given themselves. No one else suspected either.

Have you ever tried to will anything into being? Will something to happen?

It's a dangerous thing.

When all those collective minds grouped and pushed, they had already decided that they would wish certain things out of existence. Bad things. Or so they thought. They were going to make the world a better place.

Some people laughed at them, and well they might. We don't laugh now. Not those of us who remain.

That first morning, we didn't understand quite what it was that they'd done. They never quite called it prayer, because it was never an entreaty to any particular god or divine power. Every one of them, all together, they pushed within themselves.

Desire. You can feel it if you try, stirring deep there within you in the hidden places inside. Stroke it very carefully because just sometimes, it will bite. It's sly. The teeth it owns lie in your own mouth, and it can fill your head with lies.

When my sister—Joanna her name is, though she is somewhere else now, if she is still alive—and I found that there was no change, no one to help us, to tell us what to do, we decided to strike out for the city, to see if we could find anyone there. There wasn't anyone left on our street, nor the next, and if there had been, they had already left somehow, before we started to look.

The scariest thing was the quiet.

We stood at the corner, just staring into each other's faces, helplessly, hearing the absence of noise. It was the first time we'd been so conscious of the sounds that swelled in suburbia, simply by their absence. There was nothing to say. Jointly, we understood, each what the other one was feeling. Without a word, we nodded to each other, and together, headed back towards our empty home.

Our town lay on the banks of a river that curved through gentle hills, muddy and lazy in the summer heat. Clouds of insects rose and glittered in the sunshine on those gentler days, mixing faint hissing with the gentle stir of the languidly flowing water through the long river grasses. We used to play by those banks, getting muddy and laughing together as we splashed around in the mud. We knew that river well. Further downstream, it widened, tracked by a broad highway that ran to the city proper, and then, at its mouth, the clustered cranes, and containers of the city's port. We spoke about it quietly in the silence. The river was our best option. If we followed it down to the city, perhaps we would find out what had happened to the others.

We were lucky; our parents had just shopped the day before last, so the fridge was full of supplies, all of them still fresh. There were other things in the pantry. We grabbed our rucksacks from upstairs and filled them with enough for a couple of days. We reckoned it would take us that long to get to the city and find someone else to help. Joanna didn't think that we'd need anything else. The days were warm and the evenings mild and we had the river and each other. That would be enough.

What if we found no one in the city either, I asked her, but she told me that she thought that was unlikely. As it turned out, she was right.

It took us a couple of days to get to the edges of the city, to the tendrils of suburbia that stretched like roots across the open fields. We had slept beneath clear skies, the sounds of wildlife and the breeze the only things to break the silence apart from our own breathing and the few words that passed between us. Perhaps we were still in a kind of shock, but we didn't really have the urge to talk. Little by little, we were realising that that act of collective will had changed other things as well. Perhaps it was because we were so young, hadn't learned to ask the questions yet, but we accepted a lot of what we stumbled across without thinking about it. Then, and for the time afterward, we knew how things were going to be, no matter how strange they might once have seemed. The world was a very different place; that much was true. Yet, at the same time, we were a part of that new environment, along with everything else.

As we drew closer the city boundary, the road swung back to track the river's edge. Empty vehicles sat motionless in the middle, or beside the road, one or two of them at awkward angles. Buildings, small stores, and low apartment buildings grew more numerous, but still overall silence walked beside us, marking our steps. Eventually, we came upon a tall glass building blocking the road, empty now, like all the rest. A cash machine sat in the wall, and I knew if you punched in the right combination, it would withdraw with the whine of gears back into the space above, revealing a passageway through. It was amusing, I thought, that the cash machine would withdraw rather than someone withdrawing from it. A few attempts and the machine pulled back into the wall and I saw. The space was too small. I turned to her and said, "There's no way through."

"Are you sure?" she asked.

"Don't put your arm in there," I warned. "It will take your hand off."

There was nothing that told me that, but deep within, I knew, just the same way I knew that the thing would pull back into the wall and make us a part of it. Before, if there really was a before, such a thing couldn't happen.

She frowned at my words, looked into my face and she sensed my certainty and nodded. We moved away from the trap space, because that's what it was. It only took a minute more, and we found a door, glass, and steel. It was open. The building was empty, we knew. Empty, that was, except for four security guards in dark blue uniforms, shiny silver letters and numbers on their shoulders, sitting round a low table playing cards. Not one of them looked up from their game.

"Hi," I said. "Can we get through this way?" I asked, looking at the tall double glass doors behind them.

"Sure," one of them said, waving behind him casually, not looking up from his game. "There's no one left," he said.

I rested a hand lightly on his shoulder as I passed, murmuring "Thanks."

"Uh-huh," he said and pulled a card, not even looking at me. It seemed that they were resigned as we were to the new status.

What were they doing there? We did not know. Perhaps they were guarding their corporate memory, trying to still live within what had already gone. I stood and watched them for a few moments from the grassy rise behind the building, but they simply continued their game, stony faces set in deep concentration, not a word between them, as if they were afraid to speak.

I shook my head as we crossed the lawn covered slope and initially, the men, and then the building itself gradually slipped out of sight. I glanced at Joanna, and she looked back at me and shrugged.

The river ran on for an hour or so, gentle hillocks and banks where the sand and earth had broken away, leaving dark miniature cliffs along its side. Eventually, we came to another hill, somewhat taller than the rest, and the river ran around behind it. In that direction, the same way that the river turned, lay the city proper, or what remained of it. We knew that to be true. It was there in our memories, the way it had been before. Whatever they had managed to do, it hadn't touched our memory as such. Along the way, we compared things that we recalled, and reminded each other of things that we had forgotten, though Joanna remembered even more than me. It allowed us better to compare it with what was now. It had given us hope that we had seen real people. At least, we thought that they were real.

For some strange reason, our parents didn't give us pause. They were gone; we knew that much, but that was part of the natural order of things right then. Everyone was gone. Or, at least, just about everyone. I struggled with that, with the concept of what caused us, anyone, to be left behind. Was it because we were not part of that concentrated effort?

Over the rise, we came upon an old pizza parlour set low, low to the ground with sandstone walls, deserted now. Inside, everything was set close to the ground as well, nothing tall, to accommodate the closeness of the ceiling—a cosy atmosphere. We slipped inside, searching for anything that might be useful, but the place had been cleaned out. Whoever was left was fast to recognise their circumstance. They hadn't had long. Or perhaps time was all awry as well. It wouldn't take long for there to be more evidence that that was the case. Suddenly, Joanna motioned for me to be still and quiet.

"Someone's coming," she said.

At first, I thought it was the birds and nothing else. There had been a lot of birds, and I was beginning to discount them. They filled in the lack of other sounds with a sense of comfort. Though there hadn't been so much birdsong near our house. I glanced up and over the edge of one of the window ledges and I saw it there, parked on a low bank by the river, a dark red four-wheel drive, shiny but streaked with dust and I knew that she was right. It looked like it had been travelling for a long time and over a great distance. Lying still, still and we could see, there were men with a family of boys. There weren't many of them, but they stood there, surveying the surrounding area. Before long, their attention swung to the place where we hid, though there was little place for us to hide. A flock of birds came down, calling and screeching over the voices of the kids. One of the boys saw Joanna and pointed. She looked down at me and shook her head, motioning me to be still. It was then that it happened; my sister walked out towards them; her hands held out by her sides.

"I call first dibs," said the kid with the blonde matted dreadlocks. "I'll give up my morning's wages for her."

"Take her; she's yours," said the swarthy man with the black stubble. "Go get her."

She pressed her hand down gently in the air as she walked, signalling me to lie still. I lay there as the birds descended, swooping all around the cold stone interior of the pizza place. One hand was up beside my face as I lay there, barely daring to breathe, motionless, except for my eyes. I watched one of the birds, touched with red, a woodpecker. Suddenly it seemed to notice my hand, my fingers, the fingernail at the top of my index finger. The bird looked as if it wanted to peck at my nail and it made me even more scared. I couldn't cry out. I could not move. I could not do anything except lie there, for fear of alerting the men and their family of boys. My sister had walked out to meet them to keep me free. I knew that. She had known what would happen to me, what would happen to us if she let them find me. Me, I was too young and unwise in the ways of the world then to understand the full implications. Looking back, the thing that I remember most was that act of my own will that kept me from crying out, the strength that I could summon inside, because right then it mattered. And then I would remember her act of will; that must have been so much stronger. She had long gone by the time the woodpecker flew away.

Because of what she did, I eventually made it to the city, in the end, alone, but I found others there. There were only a few, but they were there.

It really mattered. I only understand now, after all this time what she did for me that day. If I could, I would take it back, will that things had happened differently. I can't do that though. There's not enough of me. I am but one. Knowing what happened back then, to all of us, because of that act of collective focus that changed our world, I cannot will it. I do not dare to will it even if I could. I can only think it.

Looking out through dusty windows, here from the place on the fifteenth floor, the sun marking gold and green outside the thick plate glass, I can sometimes see images across the water of the way the port had been, the big ships coming and going and the clusters of activity on the docks. The slick, smooth water, gilded with the touches of sunset lies still now, empty of all but those memories, and they are mere phantoms.

As I drag my gaze away from those images and stare at my fingers, where that bird had thought to do its work, I wonder what really happened to Joanna in the end. She always seemed to know so much more than I did.

San Juan's Sowing

~ *J. V. Gachs*

I've spent the last three days next to Abuela's deathbed. This morning her ragged breath finally stopped. Of all the Hermanas, I was the one she chose as her heir, and so this was my duty, but I would have volunteered for it delightedly anyway. If only to make sure she endured a ghastly death.

Each painful inhale, her fight for precious air, gave me peace, but denying her the poppy tea that could ease her passing . . . That truly delighted me. I sipped it calmly in front of her pleading eyes. Taunting her with my smile. Mocking her weeping. The woman who brought me and the Hermanas to our knees when we were children, the one who never showed a shred of mercy in the face of our blood, of our suffering, who punished our bodies, was terrified of pain, and death in her last hours. We are but tender flesh in the end, I suppose, even the ones who pretend their hearts are hard and cold as marble.

I consumed no food other than the last bread from the last harvest—as *delectable* as it sounds—as I watched her drown in her own fluids, so the numbing the tea provided was more than welcome. No one else was allowed in, a precaution to prevent her spirit clinging to the wrong vessel. All that fucking nonsense worked in my benefit for once. I put my ear close to her still warm chest and hear nothing but the emptiness of death.

I guess I'm the queen of the hive now.

Standing next to her corpse, I draw with my fingers her wrinkle-covered mouth, each a piece of the tale of a hundred years of pursed lips and spite. The mouth I've feared is harmless now. Dead meat. In the golden candlelight, the shadows of her room dance. I, then, caress mine. My skin covered with old scars. The memories of her hands stitching my lips together shower over me like summer shimmering rain. Pain seeps into my bones. I admit, the seams served their purpose that night, and so did the scars afterwards. They inspire equal parts terror, respect and lust depending on which eyes are looking at me. As the needle pierced my flesh, and the coppery taste of blood mingled with that of salty tears on my tongue, her blue eyes never once hesitated. Her wrinkled hands never trembled.

I spit on the floor beside her body before leaving the room.

"Let the girls in," I order the men guarding the door. "Abuela is dead."

"Just in time for San Juan's festival," murmurs with satisfaction one of the Padres who sit waiting in the little parlor of the Casa Grande. "Así se dijo."

"Así se dijo," repeat the others, pressing two fingers against their lips. A farewell kiss to the woman upon whose shoulders the community had once grown strong, who never admitted how weak it was now. She made sure we were protected from the outside world by the snowed picked mountains, the forests where even expert rangers get lost, the deadly river that devoured animals and humans all the same, but she failed to see our biggest threat was already within ourselves.

The Padres stand up and approach me, respectfully. One by one they kiss me on the mouth as is customary to greet the village matriarch. I recognize the taste of them all, and I despise them. These kisses are the first sign of the transition of power that will be completed tomorrow night. San Juan's Eve. The sowing. This will be the first new cycle in seventy years. Some of the Padres were children back then and barely remember Abuela's crowning ceremony. The whole community is more excited about the festival than they are upset about her death. It's going to be a once in a lifetime event. Something they will tell the children about for years to come.

Outside the Casa Grande, June's sun scorches my eyes accustomed to the gloom of the closed death room. The black-clad girls walking past me carrying white cloth, basins of water, honey, wax and a clay urn look at me curiously out of the corner of their eyes. I am the subject of their dreams and nightmares. I'll be the Abuela they will remember in their deathbeds. A mixture of excitement and fear clutches at their chests and colors their cheeks pink like bougainvillea. This is an honor for them; they have been told.

"I'm not going to call you Abuela, just so you know it, Hermana."

I turn, and Amelia is sitting on one of the stone benches in the porch of the Casa Grande. Her hair, once black and curly, is now sprinkled with gray hairs and only soft waves remain of her crazy mane. But she is just as ravishing as ever. I've seen how all the Padres look at her. Today, she hasn't put on the patch covering her empty right eye socket. There is no longer any need. Abuela will no longer be offended by the consequences of her own laws. We can show our scars proudly now. They mean we survived. They mean we grow into the Hermanas who saved the community from collapsing on itself. Amelia stands up, splitting a fig in half and offering me a piece.

"Go to hell, Sis. You look good with a clear face," I smile, accepting the red, juicy flesh of the fruit before the sun and hunger make me faint. It'd never be a good omen, less so in front of the whole town stirring to prepare for funerals and San Juan's bonfire. It's warm and sweet. It tastes different now that she's gone.

"Come on, you need to get some rest, I killed a rooster for you this morning, the fire is on." She hesitated before mustering the courage to ask: "Is she really dead? Dead-dead?"

"Dead-dead."

"Good," she replies, pulling another sweet fig out of her apron and splitting it so we can both clean the bile taste from what's coming next out of our mouths. "Out with the old, in with the new."

"Así se dijo," I reply and we both try to hide our nervous laughter from the rest of the town.

I leave Amaya sleeping in the Hermanas' room for the last time. She must be exhausted after three days of confinement with the old damned dying Abuela. The broth and roasted chicken I cooked for her will be her last meal until the old woman's honey-covered heart is served to her at the bonfire. As of tomorrow, Amaya will move into the Casa Grande and everyone will call her Abuela. Her every word will become law. Go figure. Padres following her around, memorizing, interpreting. *So it was said.* What a load of crap. It would be hilarious, though. Pity I won't get to see that.

I sit outside the house, guarding her sleep, and peeling fabes de mayo for tomorrow's feast. There's a certain stillness and joy to this morning. Abuela's death has lifted a weight from my chest. A crack in the clouds letting the sun in for the first time after years of darkness. There's hope for the future now. And I'm glad I'll be a part of the change.

I inhale deeply, as if I had been holding my breath my whole life. Kids are allowed to play and roam free while the adults prepare the funerals and the ceremony. Flower arrangements, lambs, cakes. All their busy bees' voices reach me muffled and distant.

I wonder which of those kids playing in the fields are mine. At least three must have survived. Four maybe? I'm sure one died inside me. I couldn't feel it move for a couple of weeks before the pains. And at least another I didn't hear crying, but they might have just taken it away too soon for me to hear.

I know the little girl with the pink dress and gap teeth is mine without a doubt. She is my spitting image. Sometimes I think she looks like Padre Tomás, but others I think I recognize Padre Bartolome's gestures in her tiny face. I loathe them all, so I guess it's a good thing we don't get to know who's the father so we can't blame their crimes on the children. It's already been five San Juan's bonfires since they put her inside me, and since her I have never participated in the sowing again; not as a Madre, anyway. They took that one day of being called a mother from me because I almost died pushing her out of me.

"You are a bad omen, one-eyed girl," Abuela had stated.
Yeah, like we are the problem, stupid old cow.

Amaya saved me and tethered me to this world. She brought me back and gave me a purpose. Tomorrow we'll harvest the seeds I've spread ever since. The other Hermanas told me Abuela tried to take her away from me after the birth, to keep her from healing me so she could nurture the newborns. She whipped her and threatened to disinherit her, but Amaya wouldn't budge. I believe that stubbornness was the main reason why Abuela chose her in the first place. The strong rock upon which we would build a new world. She was the only one whose lips had to be sown together, whose body had to be contented when we were teens and newlyweds in the sowing. Amaya was a force of nature and remains so to this joyful day.

My oldest will be twenty years old now. I want it to hurt if he's one of the Padres this year, but the truth is I don't feel a thing. He had it coming just like them if so. If my first born is one of the Hermanas, she will have already lived through at least four San Juan's bonfires. She might have been the one who died last year. Or one of the punished ones because they produced malformed children. Each year the number grows. When that starts to happen with the dogs, we tie the bitches outside when they are in heat so the wolves would take them and new blood would save the pack. But the Padres are greedier than dogs here. I have no way of knowing if my oldest is one of the Hermanas that sleeps in our room, or the ones that cook with us. Is she working in the fields? It's no difference.

They are all mine.

And yet none is.

"It takes a village to raise a child, so it was said."

I have always suspected that what was *said* has changed over the course of the years. There is no way to prove it of course, writing is only permitted when it comes to keeping accounts and knowing how much wheat, how many goats, how many seeds... Actually, I seriously doubt that Abuela's Abuela had any opinion about a Hermana slipping a love letter between the clean laundry of another, so I'm sure she couldn't have clearly *said* the punishment for that should be to lose an eye . . . And yet, *así se dijo* was what the Padres chanted like a mantra as they held me on my knees in front of Abuela's knife.

The Spring girls finally come out of the Casa Grande,

the big old white building at the center of our community. Although no red color is distinguishable on their
black wool robes, what is visible is how the previously
dry clothes shine soaked now. Those poor kids can't really
properly clean a chicken yet, how are they supposed to
do a good job with an old fat goat? Whatever. *So it was
said, so you have just been butchered, Abuela.* I wonder if
they managed to take the heart out. Maybe Amaya will
be having liver tomorrow instead. The thought makes me
chuckle. Some of the girls have tiny blood flowers on their
cheeks and others have puffy crying eyes. The smallest
one, who carries the urn with the heart, has vomit stained
shoes. Her hands tremble so much that the clay urn sings
against her rings. *You thought it was going to be a fun ceremony when you walked in, didn't you?*

I carry the basket with fabes de mayo in. Amaya is still
asleep. I've seen the years change her body. The pregnan-
cies, the breastfeeding, the passing of time. She's still the
same girl whose smile I fell head over heels for. I slither
inside the bed next to her, she turns around and embraces
me. Her skin is warm and she smells like sweat and poppy
tea. Her heart beats peacefully. She kisses my forehead. I
untie her gown and caress her breasts that have nurtured
so many eager mouths.

"Out with the old," she murmurs.

"In with the new," I reply while my fingers search for
her warm sex under the sheets.

☉

I shiver under Amelia's touch. She's always known how to drive me wild, or soothe my nerves. Her body and mine beat in sync.

"Bathing the new Abuela is the privilege of the Spring girls, not Autumn barren ones," Padre Bartolomé said with a disgusted grin when we left our Hermanas' house with everything ready for my purifying bath before tonight's ceremony.

"I pulled this one out of death myself just so she could serve me until the day I die, so I say now," I replied, feeling my new status fitting me like a glob.

He swallowed his words and let us on our way. Amelia pressed her lips together trying to suppress a laugh, but she let it roam free once we got to the springs.

Naked in the cold water, letting the sun warm our shoulders, we make love as Hermanas for the last time. Amelia tastes of figs and pepper. She's sweet and spicy. Tender under my touch, fierce as a wolf when it comes to defending her cubs. All our cubs. Our future. We sit together as she braids my hair with the ceremony flowers.

"Are you afraid?" Amelia asks.

"I'm more excited than afraid, I feel like I've been waiting for tonight ever since she told me I would be her heir..." I lick the scars on my lips. "Tonight will be fun, don't you think? Just be careful out there and be back on time."

"Don't worry, *Abuela*, I have it all under control," she replies before kissing me.

☉

The whole town gathers around the bonfire waiting for me to light the fire, to start San Juan's festival. The children are asleep in their beds—or spying from the windows as we used to do. The Spring girls put the red wool robe over my naked body. They draw two red stripes of lamb blood from my eyes to my chin. Blood tears for the old-world fire will devour tonight. One of them places a white clay bowl full of the same blood in front of me. I dip my feet, then my hands. It's cold. Sticky already. Its rotten stink will cling to my skin for days. I got a glimpse of myself in the mirrors of Casa Grande's Hall. I've truly become a Goddess. Beautiful but terrible, yet fair.

The Spring girls open the doors. The dim light of the dusk fills the hall. I close my eyes, and breathe in the last seconds of my old self. Once I move, there would be no turning back. My blood-stained footprints in the white cloth leading to the bonfire will be the first signs of the new dawn. I would trust Amelia with my life. I've entrusted her with our future. It all begins with this first step.

I walk out, and the Hermanas in black robes start their singing the Danza Prima accompanied by their bodhrans and tambourines. The Padres and the Madres, in white ceremonial dresses, holding each other by their pinky fingers, start dancing in a circle around the unburned bonfire. They'll go round and round and round. Faster and faster, following the Hermanas' rhythm until the song ends and they are dizzy as drunk. Their feet hurting and blood stained from stepping barefoot and carelessly on the floor while dancing.

I walk towards them. When the song ends, I break the circle and cross to the beacon. The Spring girls bring me a torch. My heart races. Not even the nocturnal birds and insects dare break the silence. I look around and there she is. As promised. Amelia is dressed in the weird clothes of the city people leaning towards the Casa Grande's wall. I could laugh at how ridiculous she looks with trousers and a black t-shirt. Red lips and eyelids as black as if she had rubbed coal on them. But the truth is she looks tantaliz-ing and dreadful, just as I do now. She's been our siren's song. There are some men with her, I can't count how many but I'm sure they will do. We only need a hand-ful. Hiding themselves poorly behind their outside world recording devices, still no one notices them. The festival has them bewitched already. Amelia nods and I throw the torch in. Heat strikes me immediately. The field turns golden. I walk towards the Abuela throne, a high wooden squared chair, from where I'm supposed to contemplate the sowing.

The Madres look at me. The fire reflects on their eyes as they wait for my signal. I clap and they all cover their faces with the ceremony clothes, as usual before letting their robes fall to the floor. They would stay put, wait-ing for the night to fall over their bodies, waiting for the touch of many hands. They would. If this was any other San Juan. Not this one.

The Padres strip off their robes too. Some already proudly show their erections and a couple of the younger ones can't resist their urges and start masturbating in the heat of the fire. There are still a few minutes to go before the sun has completely set, but they are already lost in their lust. Focused on the Madres. Distracted. Vulnerable.

The Hermanas take their places behind the Padres. They are supposed to be mere witnesses. Silent caryatides holding together the remains of the old-world, strong cold stones to build the new one upon. But tonight, I have turned them into something else. Something entirely different far more useful. Today, I have put sickles in their hands, hope in their hearts.

I have turned them into reapers.

"Tonight we do not sow children, tonight we sow blood, and we shall reap freedom. And future."

I yell the call of our people to the blackened summer sky until there's no air left in my lungs. The Hermanas slit the throats of the Padres. Not a single one of them fails or shows any doubts. It had to be done. Taken by surprise, the Padres never stood a chance. Their moans and labored breaths don't last long. Blood covers the circle around the bonfire. The Madres take their blindfolds off and dip them in the blood. They show the different stains proudly. These clothes will adorn their houses now, and be honored symbols of their new lineage.

So I have said.

Amelia was right. The filming crew hasn't batted an eye at the reaping of our Padres. They haven't even uttered a word. *Yes, Sis, good job, they will do.* The Spring girls bring me the urn with Abuela's heart covered with honey. They have done a truly lousy job taking it out. It's all cut wrong and torn. But it's ok, I don't intend to eat the damned thing. I never did.

"Tonight, a new world is struggling to be born," I scream, holding the heart in my hands over my head for all to see. "Only because the old one refuses to die. Tonight, we burnt the old to let in the new." I walk down the chair towards the fire. I make sure I step on the corpses of the Padres. They are still warm and some are twitchy. Without a word, I throw the late Abuela's heart into the flames. The Madres and the Hermanas cheer on me as I do so. It's done.

Half of it.

We all turn now to the strangers foolish enough to follow Amelia to us. The ones frozen both by fear and excitement. *We have put on a good show for them, haven't we, Sis?* Amelia was the perfect bait. Vulnerable, scarred. She's always been the best faking tears. The survivor of a cult willing to expose our practices to the outside world. Willing to give those strangers the opportunity of a lifetime. But it's them who are going to be our opportunity. Our new blood. Our future. At least, until we make sure our Madres' are with child.

Then, we'll enrich our crops with their flesh too.

So I have said.

So That Happened

~ Gerri Leen

You make your way through the gray mists to the speak-easy. Sanocles is on the door and he opens it with a bow. "My queen," he murmurs.

No one bowed to you in the above world. Danced and sang and generally made merry with you, yes. Respected . . . not so much. "You've been here long enough to call me Persephone, San."

"Yes, my queen."

"Is she here?"

"She is."

You go through and see her sitting at the bar so you slide in next to her. "E."

She doesn't look over, but a small smile plays at her mouth. "P."

No one else calls you that. And you call no one else by their initials. This is a game only you two play.

The bartenders switch out and you see it's Delphys taking the shift. Sentimental as the gray day here in Hades is long, she rushes over, takes E's hand and says, "Eurydice, I can't believe he looked back. Dumb ass."

"Yep," you say, indicating with a look she should refill E's drink and bring you your regular, and she rushes off.

You handpick your staff and your patrons from your favorites in Hades. Not from Tartarus of course. But those who amuse you from the other neighborhoods. Who seem to be a bit . . . bored with the afterlife. Those who come here to your special place are by invitation only, free to drink and dance and maybe do other things—you'd never tell what else they might get up to in the more shadowed back rooms. Staff and patrons both.

You were going to miss E terribly. It thrilled you to see her turn back, even if that idiot Orpheus had moved you to tears with his song.

A song that comes up on the playlist, and E puts her hands over her ears and says, "Make it stop."

"It's a crowd favorite. Perennial top ten. But I can understand why you'd find it irksome. Considering you left him."

E turns to glare at you. "*He* turned around. *He* blew it, not me."

"You could have said something. The entire walk, you were silent."

"And you were spying?"

"I don't have to spy since this is my realm. I see all." Your realm and your husband's. A man who everyone thinks kidnapped you. When instead you and he made a very advantageous deal. He wanted children but wasn't overly interested in love, and you wanted out of your mother's control and wasn't opposed to bearing a few children to get free. Win win. Other than his reputation of course. But then the god of the dead wasn't generally considered to be one of the good guys. A fact you used to your benefit.

He never cared. He enjoys you both for your body and your company, and he holds so loosely you have freedom to indulge yourself. Your mother, on the other hand...

E's voice is just above a whisper as she says, "Everyone here would tear me limb from limb if they knew I'd screwed things up on purpose."

"You're not wrong about that. They're in love with your love story." You touch her chin gently and turn her to face you. "Why aren't you?"

"Who says I'm not? It's a beautiful love story. Well, until the snake." She laughs but her expression holds uncertainty and you suspect you know why.

"It's ironic. No one would probably ever have cared about either of us without our men." You study her and see you're on the right track. "What's it like having everyone lauding you as part of a couple but never as yourself?"

She doesn't answer at first. Takes a sip of her drink and stares into the mirror behind the bar. You look into it too and see two beautiful women sitting close, both with expressions impossible to read.

Finally she whispers, "It's horrible. No one cares about who I am. I was the moon in the wake of his sun."

"Some would say it was the other way around. Given his obsession with—I mean devotion to you. That song moves people."

"And I get that. His music moved me too. It's why I fell

for him. It's maybe the only reason I fell for him." She
trails off as the song starts again. "Oh, come on."

You laugh and with a thought take the song off the playlist. It stops mid chorus and a new song takes its place.
There are groans throughout the bar. "Better?"

"Did you take it off forever?"

"No, but I took it off for now. Who can blame me?
You're just back. Why torture you?"

"You're way more clever than most think."

"Don't spread it around. The sweet and innocent act
gets us both a lot of mileage."

She laughs so quietly only you can hear her, and you
relish the sound, one you thought you'd have to get used
to not hearing.

Delphys brings your drinks and sets them down extra
gently, as if she's afraid the least thing will jar E into
despair. "Something's wrong with the sound system, boss.
That song . . ." She glances at E.

You give her the look that means to shut up.

"Ohhhh," she mouths and her expression warms as she
touches your hand then goes to wait on other people.

Delphys was one of your maidens. One of your favorites. Your mother didn't let you have favorites. Favorites
would have meant she wasn't your best friend, your con-
fidante, your everything. So Delphys was gone one morning and a new nymph was in her place.

That happened again and again. Until you gave up
trying to carve out a life for yourself in the above world
and turned to Hades for a way out.

"I understand what it is to be smothered with love, E." You reach for her hand and squeeze gently. "I understand what it is to be so intertwined that people don't even think of you separately, just as a duet, everlasting. The perfect daughter." You whisper the last part. "If they knew . . ."

She's squeezing your hand back much harder than you did to her. "If they knew what?"

You want to trust her, to tell her how you broke away, but this isn't just your secret. And if the truth ever reached your mother, it would break her heart—and you do love her.

But it would also probably mean you'd have to spend more time with her. And you love your freedom more.

"It's not important," you finally say and wait for her to let go of your hand but she doesn't. "What I can tell you is how much I would have missed you."

Her smile is luminous. "Yeah?"

"Yeah." You stroke her face, this lovely woman you'd thought you'd lost—but only for a time. She would have eventually found her way back.

Unless of course Orpheus sang his way—and hers—into Olympus. You wouldn't put it past him, and Hera was a sucker for faithful husbands, never having known one herself.

"You want to dance?" E is smiling in a way she never did before, open and . . . available. "Eurydice the woman is asking you. Not Eurydice the wife."

"I'd love to dance." You let her lead you onto the dance floor.

There are a lot of confused looks on the faces of the other patrons. You enjoy that immensely. They have no idea who this woman is, this lovely, intelligent, witty young thing who said not one single word to her husband as they ascended, no matter how desperately he asked if she was there. Who muffled her footsteps by hovering behind him rather than walking. Who looked less and less happy the closer they got to the above world.

"I'm glad he failed," you whisper into her ear, your breath moving her hair.

"I'm glad I made him." For a moment she feels like defiance personified in your arms but then she seems to shrink. "But eventually he'll be back here."

'Sooner rather than later if he continues to piss off the wrong women."

"Will you let him in the bar?"

"Probably not. Although I'll lose business to him. He'll no doubt set up shop in some corner of Hades and sing about you whenever you're not with him." You can feel her tense at your words. "E, down here he'll get to know the real you. Eventually, he'll have to shut up long enough to learn who you are—but you have to let him see that. It takes two to make a marriage work. And you'll learn whether you love him or just his music."

You stroke her hair as gently as you can. "It's all right to still love him."

There are times you wish your mother could be with you, could stroke your hair this way on a day when every-thing had gone wrong and tell you it would be all right.

Hades is kind, but he isn't terribly comforting. "It's always all right to still love. So long as you don't lose yourself. And you'll always have this place to escape to. I don't intend to let him in no matter how many songs he sings." Not now that you've lost her once. Not now that you know how she feels when she's close like this, holding on just right.

"No?"

"No. I'm selfish, I guess. Interfering with true love."

She pulls back just enough so you're eye to eye. "There are all kinds of true love, P."

"Yes. Yes, there are."

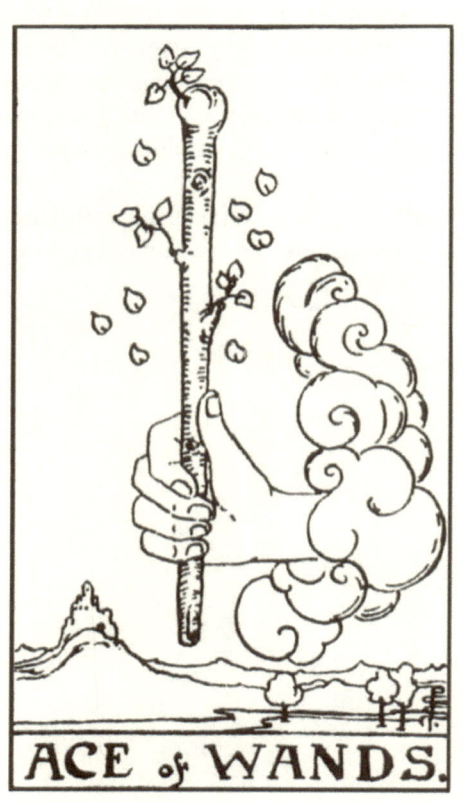

ACE of WANDS.

The Mundane Flute

~ Mark Mills

You're probably going to guess that the twist at the end of this story is that Melvin was abducted by the Old Ones because he was a terrible flutist.

That would be wrong.

Well, now that you're forewarned, you might guess that he was abducted because, although he was a serviceable flutist, he was a terrible person.

That's not quite right either. True, Melvin was a terrible person but that had nothing to do with anything. He was abducted by chance, entirely random. None of that "Chosen One" baloney. No destiny, fate, karma, justice, or any of the other meaningless words that we've created to try to wash away the random interactions of meaningless particles which is our existence. Okay, you're right that he was abducted because he played the flute, but it could have been any flutist, in any time or place. Ian Anderson, James Galway, or any other world-renown flutist that you've probably never heard of.

Oh, I may be mistaken—perhaps you do play the flute and know those artists well. In that case, I do hope you keep up with your practice. Otherwise your life has no meaning.

If you would have asked Melvin, he would have told you that, despite his years as a flutist, his life had no meaning, but, like virtually every other opinion he voiced, Melvin didn't have a clue of what he was talking about. He numbered among the few that exist as a balm to the idiot god Azathoth. Among pitiful crawling things that have formed throughout the cosmos, such as mankind and fungi, playing the flute is the only thing that has, does, or will ever matter.

Thus, when the thralls of Nyarlathotep burst into the motel lobby, ripped asunder the registration desk, and dragged Melvin across dimensions, they cared nothing for witnesses. What concern are human eyes or tongues to those that act on behalf of the living nuclear inferno?

Of course, for Melvin, the abduction was more disturbing.

Two or three—no, that's not a vague description: two of the beings repeatedly split and merged back together throughout the ordeal—dropped out of the air while he was upgrading a family of four to a room with two beds. The entities fell from the air, not the ceiling, but from a hole in reality. Slapping on the lobby tile like globs of rancid pudding, one (or two) sent tendrils through Melvin's desk, yanking it to the side. The other creature, a living clot of blood and lidless eyes, shot out a telescopic mouth and sank its teeth into Melvin's torso.

Working with the public had been no joy, but this was somewhat worse.

Melvin, soft and pudgy, put up a token thrashing in resistance before another hole in space opened about a foot above the floor. The unworldly beings leapt through it, dragging Melvin into a direction that was somehow both up and down at once.

Time had no meaning in the dimension that the creatures carried him, but it lasted forever nonetheless. Dumping Melvin in a patch of tangible smoke, they vanished, leaving only a few needle-like teeth in his shoulder.

Slack-jawed and dazed, Melvin looked around. It was space but not the space portrayed in any movie. He was sprawled in a cloud—well, that was how the movies depicted Heaven, but Melvin's clouds were black and full of razor-sharp whirling shards. This was a Heaven in serious need of an OSHA investigation.

Above or below—he couldn't tell if he was looking up or down—the sky or abyss was full of a dark star, a writhing mass of nuclear reactions, mostly the purple of a dank bruise but lined with bright, crimson scars. The comatose star had no eyes, and yet was a huge eye. It was dreaming, but sensed Melvin in its sleep. It began to babble, murmuring guttural obscenities in a language Melvin never knew he knew.

The movies lied. They said: in space, no one can hear you scream.

They were so very wrong.

"Hey, knock it off! Believe me, you don't want to wake the dead." A pale man with hollow eyes slapped Melvin across the face.

Melvin went silent mid-scream.

"You play the flute, right?" The pale man twitched as if he were allergic to the smoke around him. "You must or you wouldn't be here. Don't make any noise except music. Not unless you want that"—he jerked his chin towards the fleshy star—"to wake up."

This was far too much to take in at once—Melvin's mind was unhinged and on the brink of shattering. Fortunately, that was a common state for him.

"What is it?" he managed to croak.

"Azathoth. The creator." The pale man pointed a finger that was far too long to be human. "He made universe through his dreams. Without caring, or even being aware of us, his mind maintains all that is. We've got to keep him dreaming or it all fades away."

"What?"

"What do you mean by 'what'?"

"I mean 'What fades away?'"

"Everything. You. Me. The entire universe." The pale man's voice began to wheeze, as if unused to extended speech. "Now, shut up and start playing."

Melvin was about to protest that he didn't have his flute, but the floating shards in the smoke congealed around his hand into a perfect replica of his own instrument.

"Hurry!" The pale man stared at the dreaming god. "He's starting to stir. Play!"

Melvin didn't want to play, but he didn't want to argue either. He didn't want this Azathoth monstrosity to wake up most of all. So he lifted the faux-flute to his lips and gave it a try. It wasn't like his own flute at all—it was much better. Once he was playing, he could hear weird tunes piping all around him, melodies from alien worlds in frequencies immeasurable to man. He ignored them and played his own song, one that he'd been working on for years, about the girls in high school who had jeered at him.

It wasn't a lullaby, but Azathoth stopped his squirming, letting out a contented purr.

Melvin played his song over and over. He craved neither nourishment nor sleep. He did not, as he so often hoped, slip into a stupor, playing without thought. No, he was aware of every second, and he realized why Azathoth's guardians needed to recruit new players. After months of constant music, he heard one of the alien melodies begin to waver and then end, followed by a burst of alien bleating.

The nuclear monstrosity began to pulse and shudder; Melvin played on, ready to blink out of existence. The abhuman chittering intensified, and Melvin saw far in the distance—farther than a human eye had any right to see—a many-armed yellow beast still clutching a jade-green flute flung from the cloud, falling into the burning corona surrounding Azathoth. A final shriek, and then it burst into flames and was gone, long before it reached the mad star's surface.

Azathoth moaned. and all music devolved into cacophony. It wasn't the playing—no, Melvin, felt the notes from his flute shudder in unison with Azathoth—the universe was moving in phase with the burning void of madness.

On a cosmic scale, this was the equivalent of a child shaking his head and muttering, "No yet, Ma. Five minutes more."

All was lost. The nuclear idiot was awakening.

Then a new piping, a new musician. Melvin continued his own melody, blending it with the new song. The guardians must have abducted a new flutist, from Earth or elsewhere. It was enough. Azathoth quieted and resumed his dream.

Melvin never remembered his dreams so the loss of sleep was hardly noticed. His waking dreams had never truly gelled either. He had never aspired to become a professional musician, at least not with the flute. He only joined his high school band because his mother forced him. He hadn't practiced or even touched his old flute since May when he'd graduated high school.

He ought to play better with this one, but he wasn't. The new cloud-born flute felt like a professional model; he supposed that after tearing holes in the universe, crafting a high-end instrument wasn't much of a challenge. Yet for all its quality, Melvin bleeped and squealed as he shifted notes. The months since graduation had stripped away whatever talent he ever had.

Yet now he wanted to perfect his song. He wanted to make those girls who had mocked him cry from its sadness. He kept playing in the timeless cloud that ringed the burning idiot god. Other musicians went mad and were cast upon Azathoth's flames, but Melvin never wavered.

Was it months? Years? Centuries? No discernible changes marked the passage of time, but he knew he was getting better. His notes were strong, and his song grew until his own heart ached. He was building the sound of sorrow, but something was missing. He was so close.

So intense was Melvin's concentration that he didn't notice when the first musician collapsed to madness. The guardians rushed to replace him but then went another. And another. And another.

Azathoth's caretakers poked reality into a sieve, but they could not replace flutists quickly enough. The nuclear idiot began to mumble obscenities of quarks and gamma rays. The fabric of the universe was frayed enough that it no longer supported the very concept of music. All sound was a gibbering din—the voice of Azathoth. Soon nothing but the idiot god would remain.

"Knock it off!" Melvin's scream cut through the dying reality and stabbed Azathoth through its billions of eyes. "Knock it off! I'm coming to a break-through."

The guardians gaped as the star-sized mass of madness calmed and went still, back to its dreams of depravity and rot. Melvin's song trilled through the ether, perhaps not perfect, but so very close.

The guardians hurried to find more flutists and pipers, restoring the symphony of the cloud. It was as close to order as a universe built on disorder could be.

Some may find the twist to Melvin's story to be unbelievable. These individuals are clearly not musicians.

Box #143

~ John Klima

NEW CALDWELL UNIVERSITY ARCHIVES
BOX #143
BUREAU OF CRIME PREVENTION AND DISCOVERY
Misc papers relating to the disappearance of Oliver Wolsey

METROPOLITAN GUARD FORM #18
Requisition for OFFICERS FROM VARIOUS GUILDS of THE NEW CALDWELL METROPOLITAN GUARD and SUNDRY SUPPLIES for use by OFFICER GURNEY during the month of AUGUST 1874

- *One (1) water mage,*
- *One (1) air mage,*
- *One (1) fire mage,*
- *Two (2) earth mages,*
- *One (1) Metropolitan Guard armored transit carriage*
- *Five hundred (500) pounds of MIXED BREAD, MEAT, AND VEGETABLES*

OFFICER GURNEY assumes responsibility for the safe return of the GUILD MAGES and METRO-POLITAN GUARD TRANSIT CARRIAGE within EIGHT days of this form's expiry.

I certify that the above requisition is correct, and that the articles specified are absolutely requisite for the public service, rendered so by the following circumstances: SECURITY OF THE COMMON GOOD.

Approved by *[illegible]* on AUGUST 16, 1874.

Received at FACILITIES PLANNING the 16th of AUGUST 1874 by Officer Janis Stefanik for processing.

〜

PERSONAL LETTER
From the Private Desk of Governor Morgan Gurney

Dearest Brother:

I am disappointed and more than a little surprised to hear that Oliver Wolsey eluded capture. Eluded you, specifically. Given your voluminous accomplishments and atypical high arrest rate, I would have thought that you could apprehend a mere minor with little difficulty. Alas, the past is immutable and permanent, holding one's failure in

Box #143 53

pristine condition for future generations to gawp at and wonder how something so ridiculous could happen.

It has come to my attention that you are making a pathetic attempt to drink away the failure. Unfortunately for you, your efforts are to be focused outside the bottle. At half past eight, a carriage from the Metropolitan Guard will arrive at your address to take you to the Metro Garage. From there, you will meet up with officers from the Omega Grand Lodge whose job is to take you to intercept Wolsey and return him to New Caldwell. Our intelligence suggests that he will not disembark the ship until he reaches Broadfell.

It should not have to be said, but you are not allowed to fail in this endeavor.

I believe you will have everything you need at hand, but should you find your supplies or support lacking, I trust in your resourcefulness to discover a solution.

Sincerely,
Governor Morgan Gurney

FORMAL METROPOLITAN GUARD CORRESPONDENCE #1
New Caldwell
August 17, 1874
Chief Inspector Cromwell
Broadfell Metropolitan Guard

Sir, this letter is to inform you that Officer Marcus Gurney will be conducting an investigation into Oliver Wolsey within the City Boundaries of Broadfell. Gurney is to be given any and all assistance requested while he is in your city.

More importantly, we expect that Gurney shall not be hindered in any way by your Metropolitan Guard while on the business of the Crown.

Signed,
Sir Matthew Andy Prescott,
Viceroy of New Caldwell
Countersigned,
Morgan Gurney
Governor of New Caldwell

᠈᠆᠊

FORMAL METROPOLITAN GUARD CORRESPONDENCE #2
New Caldwell
July 1, 1854
Chief Inspector Ligarius
Broadfell Metropolitan Guard

Sir, this letter is to inform you that LIEUTENANT GURNEY will be leading an armored Naval flotilla south to Broadfell to provide succor for the attack on your port. If you are hitherto unaware of CPO Gurney and his numerous accolades, a short summary follows. Gurney has twice received the Distinguished Service Cross and once the St.

Box #143   *55*

James Cross for his show of unprecedented bravery. He has yet to lose a man under his command despite being in some of the most brutal campaigns of the Half Coup. Gurney is a consummate warrior, receiving highest marks in his company as a sharpshooter and more recently winning the Naval Forces bare-knuckle boxing competition for the fourth consecutive year.

You will be in excellent hands with CPO Gurney.

Signed,
Chief Inspector Jay Collins

>—°

Clipping from The Broadfell Times, Friday, July 7, 1854

BATHERS & FISHERMEN
ARE ATTACKED
BY A MONSTER FROM THE SEA

An eyewitness to the event claims that numerous bathers and several fishermen were attacked by a many-limbed beast that rose unexpectedly from the sea. Passers-by on the docks were alerted by the screams of the bathing ladies, and by seeing one fishing vessel pulled under the water. All those affected were found to be unharmed although many of the fishing boats in the harbor had damage to their hulls. Most damage was minor, but two ships require considerable repair.

The Broadfell Navy is investigating the incident under the direction of Broadfell's Mayor.

৵৹

Clipping from The Broadfell Times, Tuesday, July 12, 1854

NAVAL INVESTIGATION INTO SEA MONSTER ATTACK CALLED OFF

After mere days of investigation, the Broadfell Navy has called off its investigation into the sea monster attack. Hoping to use this excursion as a justification of the expense of the Navy's new steam-powered war ships, Broadfell's Navy is instead left only with HMS Hollyhock in the harbor, and that is only because the old brass-sides ship was still waiting to be decommissioned. The remainder of the once-proud Broadfell Royal Navy deployment is now an expensive decoration at the bottom of the harbor.

Loss of life was minimal, a true stroke of luck given the utter destruction of the ships.

"The creatures appeared to target the steamships," said Lieutenant Rhys O'Mangan. "We believe it was due to the noise of their engines." When pressed for more information, O'Mangan was reluctant to answer in more detail. Eventually he admitted, "Our investigation is at a standstill until more ships become available to us."

The harbor is also at a standstill as no new ships can approach Broadfell while the creatures patrol the water.

Box #143 57

Eyewitnesses describe the creatures as being brightly colored with uncountable limbs that rose abruptly from the water and tore the ships apart. Local longshoremen claim these creatures are called "Trarowr" among those who work on the ocean.

The city now waits for outside help as all work grinds to a halt.

 ⋛—ᵒ

Clipping from The New Caldwell Inquisitor, Friday, July 14, 1854

HIS MAJESTY'S NAVY TO ASSIST SISTER CITY BROADFELL AGAINST TERRIBLE SEA MONSTER ATTACKS

Upon hearing of the tragedy that occurred at the harbor to our south, New Caldwell Mayor Konstantyn Karwacki enlisted His Majesty's Navy to send a flotilla of six ships south to Broadfell.

The ships have been fitted with large iron spikes along their hulls and reinforced masts. Instead of using sails and God's air power, the Royal Navy is working with the Metropolitan Guard to use the mage guilds to reduce the two-day journey to mere hours. Mago dell'aria deliver strong gusts of air to the ships' sails while Mágos tou Neroú control the waves. An Erdmagier will be on each ship to protect the ships from the additional force of the magicked air and water. This unprecedented collaboration may lead to a new method for long-distance travel.

The flotilla is commanded by Chief Petty Officer Marcus Gurney, recently decorated with the St. James Cross. CPO Gurney is widely recognized as a rising talent in His Majesty's Navy, having led a successful counterattack in the Half Coup. CPO Gurney also completed his fourth consecutive defense of the Royal Enlisted Pugilist Championship, the first man to win more than three such championships. One wonders how CPO Gurney would fare in the Royal Commissioned Mensur Championships, but luckily for the commissioned officers, he is ineligible.

Join us in wishing CPO Gurney and his men a successful campaign in Broadfell and a swift, safe return.

꒜

Clipping from The Broadfell Times, Tuesday, July 18, 1854

ROYAL NAVY FROM NEW CALDWELL SUCCESSFULLY SEND SEA MONSTERS BACK TO HELL

Be they Trarowr or some new beast sent from Hell to destroy us for our improprieties, it took barely more than one day for Chief Petty Officer Gurney and his flotilla of Royal Navy ships from New Caldwell to drive the creatures away. The cleverly modified ships' spikes kept the creatures far enough away so that the naval artillery could fire at will. Within an hour upon arriving, CPO Gurney and his men killed three of the creatures.

Box #143 59

The assault served to goad the creatures into more attacks on the New Caldwell ships, but the deadly iron spikes limited the amount of damage from the creatures. The blood from the creatures seemed to hiss and steam upon the water while the deafening artillery fired again and again into the sea.

Rumors persist that the Royal Navy worked alongside New Caldwell's Metropolitan Guard Mage Guilds and that those same mages were at least as much a part of keeping the ships intact as the extra iron was. The ships clearly maneuvered more quickly and adeptly then ships of that size normally can. Within ten hours of entering the harbor, smaller creatures were either dead or seen swimming away.

Eyewitnesses claim that at one point a shirtless CPO Gurney dove into the water, armed only with his cutlass. The claim continues that CPO Gurney attacked the largest of the creatures and drove his cutlass deep into its eye. The creature was seen sinking into the harbor, whether to swim away or perish is unknown.

Broadfell is mightily indebted to CPO Gurney. Without his bravery and leadership, it is unlikely that the harbor could have resumed normal activities so soon.

꒱

Clipping from Pacifist Coalition News, Monday August 17, 1874

LOUPE SEEN WITH WOMAN NOT HIS WIFE,

THE SILENCE GROWING IN NUMBERS, REDHANDS LINKED TO PROPERTY DESTRUCTION IN NINE POINTS

Tenor Gilles Loupe was seen exiting The Fresh Rooftop with a gorgeous brunette who is clearly not his blonde wife. Rumors hold that the brunette was none other than Maria Vélez, a violinist with the New Caldwell Opera. Was it just colleagues enjoying a little tipple after an exhilarating performance of Viktor Sandmeier's *Vaqtning Chidamsiz Marshi*? Or perhaps this was just another in a long string of infidelity for Loupe? The singer makes the most of his prestige and beauty and is not shy from flirting with any attractive lady—or man—he runs across.

In direct opposition to the city's largest gangs—Thomas Brutus' ICE RATS and the terrifying NEW CALDWELL DEVILS—the new street gang THE SILENCE has a membership that is growing without check. It seems that more and more youths are seen every day wearing the gang's signature multi-colored cloth gag. To date, THE SILENCE have not broken any laws; they merely stand around in public in increasing numbers. The NCMG are aware of the gang but cannot act at this time.

Speaking of breaking laws, what is to be done with the recent destruction that occurred in the Nine Points? A particular sanguine-colored tarot guild is rumored to be connected to the fire in a popular downtown pub, The Beautiful Lamp. It seems the guild was looking for a young man named Wolsey and didn't let anything get in the way

Box #143 61

of their pursuit. But to make matters worse, they didn't even get their man! He escaped south to Broadfell! It is high time for the Governor to step down from his gilded seat in Parliament and do something about the rampant destruction that these tarot guilds cause in areas where people can ill afford it. (Not to mention the guilds' willful disregard for the laws of the city!) Is it up to the humble barman to cover the costs of the fire and loss of business or can the wealthy guilds be held accountable?

Clipping from Daily Beacon, Monday August 17, 1874

VICEROY AND GOVERNOR ORDER METRO-POLITAN GUARD TO FIND WOLSEY AND BRING HIM TO JUSTICE

Mere days after the Metropolitan Guard bungled the capture of Oliver Wolsey and essentially washed their hands of the case, Viceroy Prescott and Governor Gurney ordered the NCMG to close the case at all costs. The Governor is funding this endeavor through his personal accounts so there will be no additional cost to the citizens of New Caldwell.

If it was not enough that Wolsey committed cold-blooded murder, wantonly besmirching our harbor, he then brazenly stole from the respected tarot guilds. Every New Caldwell citizen knows how the existence of the tarot guilds bring near limitless prosperity and prestige to the city. One hopes that the NCMG brings its significant power to bear to ease the minds of citizens everywhere.

꩜

Clipping from The Green Street Mirror, Wednesday, August 19, 1874

WHO REALLY IS FUNDING THE NCMG'S EXCURSION TO BROADFELL?

Our humble Governor is offering his own funds to pay to send city guardsmen south to Broadfell to clean up their bungled case, but where is that money really coming from? And is this really a case for the NCMG?

Governor Gurney wants to claim that he's using personal funds, but is that money in actuality from his tax-funded salary? Or is it coming from a more unlawful source? Could our Governor be receiving money from the tarot guilds, and is that money holding sway to policy decisions? It wouldn't be the first time that the guilds benefitted from Parliamentary decisions.

Let us not forget that Governor Gurney is sending Detective Gurney, his younger brother, to handle the case personally. There are literally dozens of other detectives in the NCMG. Detective Gurney's military chest is weighed down with accolades but when was the last time he received commendation for good work done? Are the brothers working together to protect the Governor's investments?

Box #143 63

There are certainly more questions than answers at this point, but it all seems to be pointing towards corruption starting at the highest offices in the state.

ᢟ

Clipping from The Broadfell Times, Thursday, August 20, 1874

EDITORIAL

There has been a strange overturning in the popular sentiment concerning the management of public interests during the progress of the last ten or fifteen years. Previously to that time, nearly all public interests were also the interests of the communities out of whose enterprise they had grown, and foreign interference was not tolerated. If such interference was in any way attempted, it was resisted with a vigor which stopped at no means to accomplish its object of being let alone. Large sums of money are annually spent to secure vested and isolated rights, and the pleasure of local administration was supposed to be full compensation for all the expenditure which was involved in running a medium-sized city at largely the cost of large city, especially was this the case with the railroad interest.

The Crown's cities to the north, New Caldwell in particular, may provide lip service to maintaining the strength of the sea trade, but that is a mere front while they conduct their real business of trying to take over Broadfell's rail interest. New Caldwell is on an island, and as such, the expense of rail service may be too much to bear. Rather than take on their own expenses, they want to horn in on the efforts of Broadfell and reap the benefits of western expansion without putting out the initial expense.

In the midst of Broadfell's planning stages for railroad expansion, New Caldwell conveniently sends agents (officers? Mages?) from its Metropolitan Guard to our fair city. The official reason is for Lieutenant Gurney to find and apprehend a certain Oliver Wolsey who ran afoul of New Caldwell's tarot guilds. There was no reason to send agents to Broadfell; the city has its own Metropolitan Guard who are more than competent enough to arrest Wolsey and put him on trial for his crimes. This excursion to Broadfell is surely a ruse to place spies into the ranks of railroad workers and planners.

꒛

CURATOR'S NOTE:

The following are examples of il pensiero *messages. These delicate pieces of paper worked in pairs so that mages in the field could write messages on a sheet of* il pensiero *in their possession, and that same message would appear on a second sheet of* il pensiero *paper up to 200 leagues away. Mages in the field rarely had receiving paper so the messages were essentially one-way communiques.*

Box #143 65

Message #1

ATTACKED ON WAY TO MG FLEET STORAGE. OFFICER McDONALD CRUSHED ATTACKER'S CARRIAGE AT A DISTANCE THEN OFFICER GALLAGHER ENGAGED ATTACKERS BEFORE THEY COULD REGROUP. COORDINATED DE-FENSE GAVE US TIME TO GET TO MG FLEET STORAGE. WAS TOLD THE WAY WOULD BE CLEAR. WAS OUR MISSION LEAKED? EXPECT FULL REPORT UPON OUR RETURN.

Message #2

ARRIVED SAFELY BROADFELL APPROX MIDNIGHT. JOURNEY MADE WITHOUT IN-CIDENT. ROADS MOSTLY CLEAR. FEW OB-STRUCTIONS EASILY BYPASSED. CARRIAGE REQUIRES TYPICAL VIAGGIO REPAIRS. WOL-SEY SHIP TO ARRIVE IN BROADFELL TO-MORROW MIDDAY. CARRIAGE WILL BE RE-PAIRED BY THAT TIME AND MAGES READY FOR RETURN VOYAGE. TO WAIT ON GURNEY ARREST OF WOLSEY. GURNEY TRAVELED AS IF A MAGE, NO ILL EFFECTS. WHO IS THIS MAN?

Message #3

REPAIRS DONE. MAGES RESTED. GURNEY ARRIVED LATE AND W/O WOLSEY. SAID BROADFELL MG HAVE W IN CUSTODY. GUR-

*NEY HAS SEALED LETTER FOR GOVERNOR.
OFFICER PRATA TENDED TO GURNEY'S
WOUNDS BUT HE WILL HAVE A LIMP AND
A NEW SCAR ON HIS FACE. WILL REPORT TO
NCMG STATION UPON ARRIVAL.*

﹥◦

Broadfell Metropolitan Guard Officer Report
Office of the Chief of the Broadfell Metropolitan Guard
City of Broadfell
97 Washington Street
Broadfell
Sunday August 30, 1874

To the Honorable Board of Police Commissioners,

Gentlemen
The following is the 17th Fortnight Report of 1874 of
Robberies and Arrests of thieves.

• *August 17th*
William Daley arrested by Officer Valentine—
    charge breaking into his stable in Ferry Street
    near Jefferson and stealing a horse blanket.

• *August 17th*
C. N. Gerken. Grocer of 156 George St. complains
    of some person breaking into his store through

Box #143 *67*

the back window and stealing 5 boxes of segars 1 box of tobacco and 1 tin of money. Officer P.M. Breen on Post.

• *August 18th*

Redhands Guild reported another break-in at head-quarters. Nothing reported stolen. Reminded by Officer Kelly that BMG has recommended better locks for guild offices.

• *August 18th*

Mr. Chas. Schultz, Lumber dealer on the East Canal, complains of a thug harassing people on the street.

• *August 19th*

John Lewis reports that his stable was broken into and a saddle and a pair of stirrups stolen. Officer Breen on Post.

• *August 19th*

Mr. Meyers of the corner of Washington & Third Streets complains of a large man assaulting members of the public and berating them with questions.

• *August 20th*

John Murphy proprietor of The Bronze Eel's Fantasagoria Emporium on Grand Street between 6th

& 7th Streets complains of some person breaking
in and demolishing his display of tarot cards for
sale.

• *August 22ⁿᵈ*

John Hasting arrested by Officer Slattery charge
stealing a set of harnesses from Mr. Chas Schultz.

• *August 23ʳᵈ*

Confirmation from informants that Bronze Eel
break-in perpetrated by Oliver Wolsey, subject
of a HIS MAJESTY'S WANTED FOR ROYAL
JUSTICE DECREE recently delivered from New
Caldwell. Officers advised to take care in ap-
proaching Wolsey.

• *August 25ᵗʰ*

Officer Valentine detained NCMG Officer Marcus
Gurney for acting outside his jurisdiction while
searching for Wolsey. Officer Valentine recognized Gurney from boxing posters from his
youth. Due to his heroic efforts in 1854, which
likely saved the city, BMG has dropped all charges
against Gurney.

•*August 26ᵗʰ*

Mr. L. Weinthal complains of some person stealing
3 dozen vests from his store 56 Washington St. by
breaking in his back window. Property recovered.

Box #143   *69*

• *August 27ᵗʰ*

Oliver Wolsey arrested by Officer Valentine on complaint of John Murphy. Wolsey also found to be in possession of several items of contraband. Wolsey will be extradited to New Caldwell after he is processed and arraigned in Broadfell.

• *August 28ᵗʰ*

Officer Marcus Gurney remanded to return to New Caldwell. The case of Oliver Wolsey is now above his and our jurisprudence.

Respectfully Submitted
Sean H. Howard
Broadfell Metropolitan Guard Assistant Commissioner

17th Fortnight Report of 1874 by Assistant Commissioner Howard of Robberies and Arrests of thieves.
Presented read and received and filed
Sept. 8th, 1874
Nath. A. Robertson
Clerk

⊃~

Arrest Report Broadfell Metropolitan Guard
CONDITIONAL ORDER of LICENCE to a MALE CONVICT made under the Statutes of His Majesty King Albert VII.
Broadfell
28th day of August 1874

HIS MAJESTY is graciously pleased to grant to Oliver Wolsey who was convicted of breaking & entering and destruction of property at the Bronze Eel Fantasagoria Emporium for the City of Broadfell on the 20th day of August 1874 and was then and there sentenced to be kept in Penal Servitude for the term of two weeks and is now confined in the Long Bay Correctional Center.

HIS ROYAL LICENSE to be at large from the day of his Liberation under this Order during the remaining portion of his said term of Penal Servitude, unless the said Oliver Wolsey shall, before the expiration of the said term, be convicted of some indictable Offence within Broadfell, in which case such License will be immediately forfeited by Law, or unless it shall please His Majesty sooner to revoke or alter such License.

This License is given subject to the Conditions endorsed upon the same, upon the breach of any of which will be liable to be revoked whether such breach is followed by a Conviction of not.

HIS MAJESTY hereby orders that the said Oliver Wolsey be set at liberty within Thirty days from the date of this Order.

Given under my Hand and Seal,
Governor Tristram Geddings
Under Authority of His Majesty King Albert VII

꒰ꙫ

Box #143   71

Sealed Letter for Governor Morgan Gurney

Dear Governor Gurney:

It gives me no small pleasure to send this letter. By the time you receive it, your brother should be back in the fold and Wolsey headed north via train under armed guard. Do not congratulate your brother, however; he did more to obstruct our inquiries into Wolsey's activities than not. Once we detained the younger Gurney, we were able to proceed post haste in the capture of Oliver Wolsey.

This was accomplished with no interference from outside Metropolitan Guard and no interference from tarot guilds. From what I hear, this is quite different from how things are handled in New Caldwell. It is my personal opinion that you allow your guilds too much freedom in the governance of your city.

Had I received your letter in a timely manner, perhaps we could have worked with Officer Gurney. As it was, we thought there was a new gang in Broadfell, mucking about town banging people in the head and asking questions. But no, it was just your half-trained bulldog, as is usual, solving problems with his fists rather than his brain.

Your letter, terse and too informal, arrived after your brother. While Broadfell does not measure up to the cosmopolitan nature of New Caldwell, we are in possession or more than a little funding and have access to modern technology such as *il pensiero* messaging and the telegraph. Either would have worked in getting a message to us if expediency was desired. If apprehending Wolsey was as important as you suggest, surely no expense should have been spared?

Nevertheless, we have Wolsey in custody. We will process him for the crimes he committed in Broadfell and then release him to your care.

We respectfully ask that New Caldwell refrain from interfering in Broadfell concerns in the future.

Yours lovingly,
Chief Inspector Cromwell

>—•

Clipping from The Broadfell Times, Monday, August 31, 1874

DARING ESCAPE!
WOLSEY ELUDES TRANSFER
TO NEW CALDWELL

An enormous explosion shook the Broadfell Central District Metropolitan Guard station in the early hours before dawn. Smoke lifted in willowy wisps from the area where custody cells are located. The outside wall was breached from inside Oliver Wolsey's cell.

The bunk of the cell was turned on its side likely to shield Wolsey. A tight circle of charred marks was etched into the stone floor of the cell near the destroyed wall. Our sources indicate that the marks are the size and shape of tarot cards.

Box #143 73

Currently Broadfell Metropolitan Guard have released no information on the whereabouts of Wolsey or of their plan for his abduction. *The Broadfell Times* will have an update in our noon edition.

PAGE of WANDS.

From a Serpent, Jade Bentasillus

~ Reggie Kwok

To Whom It May Concern,
I would like to express my interest in the Entry Game Designer Position at Slay Them All Games. I discovered this job through Monsterous.com. I am a serpent from Mammoth Cave in Kentucky.

I obtained my B.F.A in Animation from Scab University. My individualized internship at the indie company, Dontblink Entertainment, exposed me to several talented beings working in animation. In collaboration with others at this indie company, I demonstrated my creative and communication skills within the award-winning video game, *Life Is Scales.*

My portfolio is available at Fromagreenserpent.com. I am willing to relocate to California if accepted for this position.

From a Serpent,
Jade Bentasillus

☉

Dear William Banker and John Smith,
Thank you for the in-person interview on January 28. I enjoyed discussing the plans set for this company.

My portfolio contains several demo videos and images. In the attachment marked sample project, the characters delve into the meaning of the twenty-first century dragon. They encountered many situations in both urban and rural environments, and the list of assets from my portfolio can assist in creating an environment that anyone can enjoy regardless of species.

Every dragon has an element, and I am no different. My parents' breath magic related to health and medicine led to my own ability to produce cough drops on a whim. Co-workers will never go cough-drop-less ever again. I left a jar of mint and thyme cough drops with the secretary as a gift.

I am interested in this position. As requested, I have enclosed my references as an attachment. I am eager to work with you. I am available via DRAGON SHOUT, the translation slash email app, and email.

From a Serpent,
Jade Bentasillus

☉

Dear John Smith,
Why do humans respond to me via DRAGON SHOUT when I am able to type using several sticks strapped

around my ten claws? I've increased in proficiency over the past few years, and I demonstrated my typing skills in front of the entire company. I don't understand why I am assigned to these typing tasks when other humans from this exact company cannot type with all ten fingers. Yes, I've seen at least one person using the two-finger strategy.

Every time that I listen to some fake dragon noise echoing from DRAGON SHOUT, my hearing orifices cannot take it anymore. I have been waiting to find a human who can actually speak in dragon tongue. No human from the company can solve this problem.

However, I need several solutions to move into place. First, the cubicles are too small for me. My co-worker has to work in the break room while I'm taking up the space of two cubicles. Everybody stares at me while I'm working.

Second, these human computers aren't working for me. I've been breaking these keyboards and computer screens left and right, and one time, I broke the ceiling from a surprise. You three expect me to pay for the six pieces of technology, which is unacceptable.

I'm not going into details until I receive a response. I don't understand why nobody responds to my emails.

From a Serpent,
Jade Bentasillus

☉

To: William Banker and John Smith
From a Serpent: Jade Bentasillus
Subject: A Report on the Outrageous Discrimination
against Dragons and Rectification Measures
Date: February 1

The purpose of this memo is to declare how outdated and dumb human memos are. Why haven't you responded to my emails? More importantly, why is there this require-ment to submit complaints in this format? The true pur-pose of this memo is to offer strategies against interspe-cies discrimination.

Incident #1: The Typing Assessment

The madness all began on day one. For some reason, the company asked for a demonstration of my typing ability, and I was willing to demonstrate this through my lovely ten sticks designed to interact with technology without blowing it up all the time. However, co-workers planned for this event, for the whole office flocked to witness the typing dragon.

This simple exercise transformed into a game where co-workers demanded that I type until my fingers were ready to rip the keyboard in half. Co-workers were bet-ting money on whether the dragon could type simple sentences humans could write.

After typing ten pages, I stopped.

According to the employee handbook given on the first day on my desk, the company prohibited gambling for all employees. I demand a very public announcement reminding others of company policy. I expect the supervisors to enforce this policy.

Incident #2: Modeling

At first, I thought that I was providing a decent service for my fellow workers by providing a proper image of a dragon. A co-worker asked me to enter her office one day and to strip down my clothes to the bare minimum for dragon anatomy practice. To protect the worker's identity, I chose a rather fitting name, Steak.

Steak went straight to work with her drawing and scribbled on her tablet at a very fast rate.

But then her tablet flashed once at my crotch.

She swore and thrust the tablet toward another direction.

I asked, "Since you have a picture of me, may I have my clothes back?"

She said, "Not until I shoot your face."

She proceeded to take more pictures. When I reached for my work clothes, she shoved them into the office drawer. I chopped the desk in half and then grabbed the clothes. I ran straight for the nearest bathroom. William Banker spotted me naked and gave a verbal reprimand when I was fully clothed. I was not even able to explain myself because the boss did all the talking and none of the listening, and I refuse to repeat the words that he said to me.

Incident #3: Interruptions for Cough Drops

I am unable to concentrate on work at the office. The cubicle doesn't cover half of my height. Every fifteen minutes, a co-worker taps my body and asks for a cough drop. I've placed visible signs all over my cubicle to drink water. My cough drops are not a cure all for colds.

Let me explain a little bit about dragon breath. Every time I breathe cough drops, I feel a little sick. With co-workers asking for cough drops every fifteen minutes, that's a total of thirty-two times a day when I feel like vomiting. For a whole three days, I had to call in sick due to my very own nausea, cold, and fever.

Then, the co-workers began slapping at my back the morning that I arrive on sight waiting for their free cough drops.

Incident #4: The Saddle

I received a gift with brown wrapping paper and a black bow on my desk. I unwrapped it with a neighboring co-worker and many more flashing their smartphones toward me. I even paused to ask them a question about the gift, but they didn't respond and continued to record.

They gave me a horse's saddle. They proceeded to pin me down and to attach the saddle against my will. I tried to resist, but I was outnumbered and outmatched. They also recorded themselves riding on top of me.

Incident #5: Paying for Office Equipment

I received a bill and a citation for the office equipment designed for humans. I am refusing to pay it.

Instead of buying the same thing for a dragon that he could crush every time, why not buy a decent sized computer with a dragon proof keyboard, so that every being can work without threatening one's wallet.

I am willing to provide resources on proper human-to-dragon interaction and etiquette. Please respond in a day's time.

☉

Dear Abby Tuffer,

Thank you for our lunch and meeting on February 10. Speaking to another serpent relieves me of every pound of headache from other co-workers. I've learned much from your portfolio. I'm interested in how the art and the game design combine together in the portfolio.

I cannot help but to point this out. During our lunch at the local coffee shop, a group of four teenagers pointed at a dragon.

One of them said, "Go back to China, where you belong!"

The poor dragon did not have features of an eastern dragon: no whiskers or slender body. In fact, the dragon looked like a western dragon with wings at the back and horns. Humans can be so offensive.

I said during our meeting that I would give the details to my meeting with the supervisors via this email, for, as I mentioned, that it did not go so well. In fact, everything went horribly wrong, to the point where if I ever were to mention specific names, I would wind up in another netherworld filled with trouble.

For starters, one of the supervisors decided to call me a snake for even requesting this meeting in the first place. From then on, I knew that they weren't going to do anything about my issues. The employee, Steak, denied all of the sexual assault accusations that I made against her. The supervisors placed my cough drop making as an additional duty, as if I was the official cough drop maker of the company. They regarded the horse saddle incident as absurd. They said that some insurance covered the damage done to the office equipment, but in the end, they still deducted extra money from my pay stub.

I have no faith in this company at all.

I want to eat my phone because nobody is responding to my emails.

From a Serpent,
Jade Bentasillus

⊙

Dear Abby,
I got your package of six plastic bobble heads in the mail today. Did you really make these for my office? I'm not

sure if the humans would approve of naked humans wearing underwear as hats and T-shirts as pants. Instead, I keep them in my apartment, where I flick my claw at them every time I feel like eating an office worker.

By the way, the whole I-ate-somebody-for-a-whole-two-minutes thing is a complete hoax and fiasco. The same bitch who took a picture of my crotch decided to Photoshop herself into my snout. The supervisors believed her, and now they are talking about dragon muzzles to protect human lives.

I'm on paid leave for a week.

Before I left, we were talking about the new dragon hire that was supposed to have a programming job but earned the design position since "he was a dragon." We spat out twenty different ideas during our last lunch before going on leave, and we agreed to keep the top four ideas in an email.

1. Check his portfolio. One or two of us should teach him the ropes to animation since they think that all dragons are artistic scholars for some reason.

2. Convince him to come to our two lunch spots at the pond and the coffee shop.

3. Support him during the typing assessment. Everybody is going to be there. With the power of two dragons, perhaps our growls and protests can end the taunting and the gambling.

4. I should remind him never to serve as a physical model. They have digital pictures on the Internet for a reason.

That could assist the new hire with blending into a toxic work environment.

From a Serpent,
Jade Bentasillus

☉

Dear Tobert Dell,
Welcome to Slay Them All Games! As a fellow coworker and dragon, I would like to offer a tour of the building to meet the other co-workers.

One of the supervisors may request a typing assessment as a part of company protocol. Given the programming background, I trust that this can go well. Abby, the other dragon co-worker, and I can check the surroundings of the testing area. This is a private affair after all.

I've set up a learning module on Fromagreenserpent. com. I would complete this module within the week. After the week, I must remove it. I don't want the supervisors and bosses to know what I'm up to.

If anybody asks you to serve as a model, I would say no and go elsewhere.

Could you accept Abby's invitation for lunch at the local coffee shop? We have a lot to discuss, including work culture, fellow employees, and much more.

From a Serpent,
Jade Bentasillus

☉

Dear Tobert Dell,

On behalf of the company, I would like to apologize for the incident on May 16. It was the last straw when they asked us to stop using the human bathrooms.

Abby and I didn't understand the cost to all of the electronic gifts. The entire electrical surge came from your ability to barf electronics. Abby and I share the same weakness of becoming sick after using our breath magic, so we assumed the same for you. We would like to apologize for our mistake.

The electricity popped two light bulbs and almost set the lampshade on fire. Lucky for us, two other employees, a female and a male, assisted with putting out the fire, but the female employee complained about the dung-like odor.

She said, "One of the dragons pooped in the break room."

The female and male human left. Then, one of our bosses decided to escort all three of us to the lawn so that we could go to the bathroom.

This was so wrong. I felt like eating the boss and telling his family that I ate him, so that way, I could go to jail to protect myself from all of this hatred. It never made sense.

We don't have to deal with this. We have to talk.

From a Serpent,
Jade Bentasillus

⊙

Dear Steaks,
As of June 1, Jade Bentasillus, Abby Tuffer, and Tobert Dell are resigning from our positions.

From the dragons,
Jade Bentasillus
Abby Tuffer
Tobert Dell

⊙

About This Game:

Dear potential employee,
Congratulations! Out of the fifty thousand jobs available on the Internet that are clearly advertisements, you stumbled upon the most important thing in the world: work. When dragons have taken over every possible job possible, learn about the meaning of this activity called work.

GET A JOB
Take a job as a button presser, a saliva spitter, a taste tester, a vomiter, or six other fabulous opportunities. Remember, the ability to eject bodily fluids is a requirement.

FLY TO WORK
Use your wings to fly to work. Cry when you real-
ize that you don't have wings. Listen to authorities
complaining about your lack of wings.

HAVE A LIFE
Stressed about work? Leave! Plenty of other op-
portunities provide real spambots bombarding the
internet with advertisements for restaurants and
retail stores. Search for a new job.

The first thousand customers who purchase this
game will receive an exclusive puke bucket from
Tufferware!

From Dragons United,
Jade Bentasillus
Abby Tuffer
Tobert Dell

☉

Tufferware Teams up with Dragons United to Pro-
mote VR Game

Dear fellow consumer,
Tufferware assists Dragons United, a new indie company,
with promoting Dragon Job Simulator, a new virtual reality
game on Volcano's PC gaming platform, Lava. Gamers can
experience the true meaning of work in a dragon society.

Tufferware is teaming up with GamePit to display the power of virtual reality through several demos throughout the stores. GamePit.com contains a map with all of the possible demo spots available.

Tobert Dell, founding chief architect and coder, describes the origins to the game: "It all started when we all agreed to quit our jobs. We started to spit out ideas, which turned into us spitting random objects out our mouths. After our brainstorm, Tuffer and Bentasillus were sick for a whole week, and I had to avoid technology for a whole day to remove the electricity out of my body. The next day, I received an email from Bentasillus containing a document with a novel's worth of ideas."

Dragons United began in response to policies from Slay Them All Games, a company preparing to declare bankruptcy from poor sales. The three founding dragons all worked in one apartment to create this game.

Abby Tuffer, founding creative game designer, states, "It was a dark time, having three dragons in a two-room apartment. One of us would often sleep on the floor or would continue working while the other two shared the same bed. While working on this game, I contacted an uncle who knew the CEO for Tufferware. I pitched the game to the CEO, who laughed so much that he needed several tissues to remove the tears from his face. Our lives changed so much after that point."

In *Dragon Work Simulator*, the gamer plays as a human who is searching for a job. Several occupations require the human to spit objects out the mouth and to carry a puke bucket, the same bucket that Dragons United designed and Tufferware manufactured. The puke bucket received many comical reviews on Forest.

"Depending on identity, the game can become really dark," states Jade Bentasillus, founding art director, "but any being, human or dragon, can enjoy this game. After all, the game came from personal experiences from our previous jobs. Once we received news about both Game-Pit and Tufferware supporting us, I promised my founding members that we would never have to worry about a second job ever again."

Dragons United reported that *Dragon Work Simulator* is updating until fan support dies down. With high demand for the puke buckets, Tufferware and Dragons United are working together to produce and to promote the famous bucket found in the game.

Starfish Sister

~ *Jon Lasser*

Riley's dops lay scattered across her desk. They stretched their tiny legs and arms, sitting or reclining, miniatures of her down to their tiny, exasperated sighs as they studied.

One dop crammed for tomorrow's biology exam—nothing about evolution, Father would be relieved to hear—while others studied quadratic equations or caught up on the Honors English reading, which was—well, she'd find out soon enough. Her social dop chattered away on the cloned phone, gossiping with Sophia and Purvi and Olive about boys or school or maybe both at the same time. Two dops bounced on the blade of a jam-sticky butter knife as though it was a springboard. What were they supposed to be doing?

As hard as Riley tried to keep all the dops on task, the aroma of Mom's roast chicken wafted up the stairs like it was trying to distract her. Her stomach growled, dinner having been one slice of toast with the thinnest smear of strawberry jam spread over it, and how could she focus with the dinner-table conversation echoing through the vents? Every bit of it, from Father intoning grace like the whole congregation was present to Mom's inane questions about school, felt calculated to drive her mad.

Roast chicken was her favorite meal, too, but if she didn't babysit all the dops, she'd be up past midnight with homework. Without her watchful eye, they'd stop working and whisper to each other like they were planning a mutiny. It was probably just high spirits, a mirror of her own reluctance to engage with the work, her own capacity for distraction.

And so Beta, who never appeared distracted, sat downstairs with Riley's family, eating dinner instead of doing PSAT prep or applying for internships or whatever. Mom spoke to the dop in that low, soothing tone that always gave her the heebie-jeebies, even from upstairs. Riley was jealous of how Beta felt nothing when talking with her parents, and how she managed to be so organized. Other than that, Beta was so like her it was eerie; Mom couldn't suspect anything.

"And then Miss Koolhaus took a pin and poked Manish from behind," Beta said, "Where he couldn't see, and the air all went out of him." She must've gotten the story telepathically from the social dop, but Beta was selling it like she'd seen it herself. Riley was jealous: if only she could hear the dops in her head as clear as the voice of God, the way they could hear each other!

"I'm glad *you* don't send a dop to school," Mom chuckled. "Imagine the embarrassment if you got caught!"

"Getting caught isn't the point," Father grumbled. "It's the difference between right and wrong—"

"But I'm not," Beta said, "So there's nothing to worry about." It was true, mostly. Beta wasn't sending anyone anywhere, and Riley usually went herself, Phys Ed excepted. Riley was in charge, if not always in control. But what teenager was? How *could* you be in control when your parents ruled your life, when you didn't know or couldn't admit who you were, and there were so many of you running around, each one spreading you out just a little bit further?

"—like the whole question of dops," Father continued, steamrolling Beta the way he would have steamrolled Riley, or anyone else. "They're a perversion of natural law."

"Yes, Father," her dop mumbled. The poor thing shouldn't have to put up with his Biblical reasoning, even though dops didn't have feelings or thoughts of their own. If Father knew what Riley was doing, he'd disown her, or worse.

Father took dops seriously, even if most of his flock were a bunch of hypocrites. Who among them hadn't set a dop to watch an episode of *Mr. and Mrs. X* so they could chit-chat about it at work on Monday? Whatever Father said about "natural law" while they nodded in their pews, however they parroted his homilies in public, their dops watched a show about dops written and acted in by dops so they'd have something to talk about with their coworkers—or their coworkers' dops. None of them batted an eyelash at the Army's dop platoons, each orchestrated by a single master, thinned by her effort to little more than the desire for victory.

Somehow, like drinking beer or smoking weed, adults thought only other people had a dop problem. Never themselves. Dop dependency might be like sex addiction: only a problem if you believed in it. Say if you went to a church like Father's. Dops weren't a problem for Riley as long as she didn't get caught, and as long as she could keep them in line.

"All done." Her math dop sounded reluctant, like she wasn't ready.

Riley sighed. She wasn't ready either. The dop hopped across the bed, til she got stuck between two large folds of the comforter. Riley picked her up and held her in her palm.

She popped the math dop into her mouth and bit down.

Something went squish. Tiny bones cracked as Riley chewed. She swallowed. She felt a jolt, like touching a nine-volt battery to her tongue, and tasted metal halfway down her throat. Her belly grew warm, like she'd just downed a Jello shot of experience. Quadratic equations weren't that hard. It was just cross-multiplication, if you thought about it. The warmth spread through her, creeping up her hands and her neck, rushing down into her legs and toes and everything else. It was as though she'd written the equations herself, over and over, until it came naturally.

She chewed through her homework: the parts of a cell, *Of Mice and Men*, how Franco's Spain served as an ideal model for America, the effects of vitamin B-6 on the human body. If dops were against the rules, why did school have a college prep curriculum so rigorous that nobody could possibly keep up without them?

Her Phys Ed dop wasn't home yet. That was one class Riley didn't need to attend, even if she had to blow up that dop like a thick-skinned balloon. Since making full-sized dops was a pain in the behind, she always used them twice—once for work, and once for fun. After class, she'd sent it downtown for dinner and clubbing. What Riley would do, if she could get away from babysitting her dops long enough. If she wasn't worried about getting caught.

Her stomach gurgled queasily, glutted on knowledge. No time to think about it. She cleared off her desk and put the mat down, the slice of toast she'd filched from downstairs on top. Four plus Beta would be enough for tomorrow, so she cut it into quarters. With a sewing needle she put a drop of blood from her thumb on each, and applied the compound from the dropper. The toast softened back into bread, folded in on itself, and took her shape. The dops rolled onto their backs and cried out like babies. She blew gently across their tiny faces until they stopped crying and fell asleep.

The window rattled, but it was only the wind. Not her dop come back with the forbidden taste of rum and coke, or even another woman in her mouth. Riley was too wiped out even for mom's chicken, so even though she knew she should wait up for PE, she left the window unlatched and turned off the lights.

☉

Something outside crashed and Riley was out of bed, her head out the window peering into the darkness, before she knew she'd woke.

Father's footsteps boomed as he tromped downstairs. The outside lights came on.

"Who's there?" His church voice, the one he used when he was afraid but ashamed to admit to his fear, reverberated in the darkness. The voice Riley heard in her head even when he wasn't mad, the voice when she imagined talking to him about what she really felt, what she really wanted. Not more college prep, not church.

There her dop was, around the corner from where Father was looking, sprawled face-down in the mulch below the pine. Its arms pinwheeled round like a starfish and cast strange shadows in the light of the full moon. No wonder she hadn't seen it right away. It must have fallen from the tree, climbing up to her window. Riley's stomach turned: she should have stayed awake. If she got caught—

"I'm calling the police," Father bellowed. The church voice probably meant he hadn't seen anything and was bluffing, trying to put a scare into whoever he imagined was outside, threatening their perfect little lives. If only he knew what went on inside the house. Not only Riley's dops. Father still talked about how he wanted a son, that he had never wanted Riley to be an only child, but he didn't seem to understand there was a reason she didn't have any siblings. Mom had never said a thing but Riley knew how to put the pieces of a secret together.

She held still for what felt like ages until Father clomped back up the stairs. His bedroom door slammed and his bed groaned. Mom said something Riley couldn't make out through the wall. Soon he was snoring.

The stairs hardly creaked as Riley tiptoed down. She slipped on her shoes. The alarm chirped once as she opened the back door—darn, she hadn't thought about that. Too late now.

Where was the dop? She turned the corner, toward her room. Her phone's flashlight threw shadows of shrubs and planters that made everything feel faraway and strange.

There it should have been, furrows in the dirt in that sprawled-out shape. Footprints led away, into the grass.

The drainpipe shook. Her dop was climbing back up again. It must have come to while she waited for Father to fall asleep, waited in the grass and come back. She could almost taste it, a marshmallow of sin. It would be soon.

The dop shimmied back down, toward her. No! Had it seen her? Why not wait inside? They couldn't go back in together—someone might see them like that. Besides, she'd set off the alarm. For all she knew, Father was on his way downstairs again with the shotgun. They needed to climb the tree, quick.

"I'm Beta," the dop said as its feet landed in the mulch, as though it sensed her confusion. "P.E. booked it down the block. Let's get her."

Riley had never lost a dop before. Now and again, in their "Scared Straight" assembly, school would show video of people who'd lost too many dops. All those parts of themselves vanished, what remained staring blankly at the camera, emptier than any dop. She didn't want to be like that.

And then she understood: this was it. Beta and PE had it in for Riley. They'd plotted against her. Of course they had. Beta would eat Riley and replace her. It's what Riley would have done, if their positions were reversed. It was all right: Beta deserved better. She was smarter, more ready for college, better under deadlines, more in control of their shared life. Besides, Riley couldn't eat Beta, not any more. She was too big to eat whole, and Reilly hated dop soup.

"You go inside," Riley said. "In case my parents check in." Best to pretend she knew nothing.

Beta shook its head. "You'll need my help to catch her. Let's go."

It strolled across the lawn to the sidewalk and started to jog down the block, towards the main street. Riley reached the pavement and ran, too.

Mrs. Winfield stuck her head out her bedroom window and clucked loud enough for Riley to hear. She'd no doubt mutter about "witchcraft" at church on Sunday after shaking hands with Father, even though Riley had seen Mrs. Winfield making sandwiches at the soup kitchen the same time she was at home glued to the boob tube, even though her daughter Everly's dop sat right next to her in Miss Koolhaus's class. Mrs. Winfield had art on her walls from that dop artist, the one Riley saw the clip about in art class, with the factory where all of him painted the same picture at the same time.

"This way," Beta whisper-shouted, gesturing at the alley. "Hurry!" Riley wiped the sweat from her brow and heaved another breath. Maybe she shouldn't have skipped so much PE.

Riley spun on her right heel to turn. This was as good a place as any. She fell and yelped as though in pain from a twisted ankle, steeling herself for the judgement she was owed.

"Over here," the dop shouted. "She's fallen!" It stood above her as P.E.'s footfalls grew near.

Riley's heart beat faster even though she lay flat on her back, the asphalt smooth and warm below her.

They looked down. Beta—at least, she thought it was Beta—smiled, and pulled a steak knife from her belt.

"This is the part where you tell me how I've hurt you," Riley said. "The part where you stab me with that knife and turn me to soup." She shrugged, though the tar sort of stuck her in place. "Get on with it."

Beta shook her head. "I don't like dop soup any more than you."

"How will you eat me? Piece by piece?"

Riley wanted more than anything to be whole—whether it was in her own body or Beta's didn't matter so much. Some head-shrinker might think she wanted to die, but that wasn't it: she wanted to be herself—her best self, the way Beta was—to herself and her friends and her parents.

Even so, she shuddered at the thought of being eaten, no matter how many dops a week she ate. That was different—wasn't it?

"I'm not here to kill you. I'm here to free you." Beta stabbed P.E., then pulled the knife up to slit its neck. The blood fell like warm rain on Riley's face. She licked it and shuddered with the feelings that arose. P.E. collapsed. Beta fell to her knees next to P.E. and sawed off a finger. She ate one, then fed the next to Riley.

Riley recalled running her finger along a woman's leg, her finger tracing the silky line where the other woman's panties stretched over her dop-soft flesh. The woman moaned with pleasure. Riley moaned too, remembering.

"I don't deserve to live." Riley sobbed. "I'm—"

"The Hell you don't." Beta stared into her eyes. "We're the same. Not abominations. Not broken."

"How—"

"We have the same father." Beta nodded. "I never could hide from the knowledge of what he thought of me. Sure, I could keep my mouth shut at the dinner table, just like you, but I couldn't pretend to myself that I wasn't a dop." She bit her lip, just the way Riley did. "I had to sit there, dinner after dinner, seething inside while he called me an abomination. Said I was a sin to my face.

"But I knew better. If you cut the legs off a starfish and toss them back into the ocean, each leg becomes a new starfish. I'm your starfish sister. If you have a soul, so do I. No matter what he said, I knew I was no sin—at least not because of the way I was born.

"You—well, thanks to Father, you never were sure I wasn't Satan's spawn. If—"

"I never said—" Riley shook her head.

"You didn't have to. I know you, Riley. I know your thoughts."

"All of them?" It couldn't be. Beta had to be lying to her. Dop telepathy didn't extend upwards, only outwards. That's what people said. But maybe the dops had lied to them?

"All your thoughts. Including the ones Father believes are violations of God's will. Abominations. Even if he doesn't yet know about you."

Riley wiped tears away from her eyes, but said nothing. Maybe Beta wasn't lying. Maybe they weren't so different.

"It's okay, Riley." Beta knelt over her and wiped the blood from her face with a hankie. She sucked the cotton until only the slightest trace of pink remained. "I'm not an abomination. You aren't either." She kissed Riley on the forehead.

Both girls sighed. Riley choked back a sob.

"You killed her. If you're my starfish sister, then so was P.E."

"She was just started. You grow into your soul over time, the way a starfish leg takes a long while to become whole again. Trust me, it's different."

Riley shook her head, not believing but wanting to. It was just what she would have said in Beta's place.

"Even if I was lying, which I'm not, it's too late anyway. Just one more dop, right?" Beta pulled Riley to her feet.

"Now what?"

"Now what?" Beta repeated, laughing: she hadn't thought so far ahead. Riley was getting a little of that dop telepathy after all.

Without asking each other, Riley and Beta faced downtown.

"Now we run."

And the two sisters, alike as twins, disappeared into the night.

Wolven

~ Daniel Dagris

Ellis dismounted his horse and joined the men already scalping the dead. Remnants of a small tribe, most of its men probably already killed in one fight or another. Blood soaked into his clothes and dried on leather meant to keep the western sun and arrows from biting too deep. Wiping gore from his forehead, Ellis was insulted to share a promised land with superstitious folks who blew across it like autumn leaves, but also glad for the sport of it. He pressed one nostril with a bloody thumb and blew out of the other a considerable amount of congestion.

The men built a fire just out of sight of the day's massacre as night took hold. Bedrolls were loosed and bellies filled. A few hats rested on saddles while others held back the tide of firelight from men drifting to sleep, mid conversation. Shadows shrank from the blazing fire, flickering a comedy of demons, teasing and chasing about. As the fire matured, the demons inched out along the sand, towering longer than any man sitting against a rock or curled up sleeping.

Ellis awoke and wandered away from the orange glow. His pistol hung loose on one finger as he gripped his works and relieved himself. Finished, he turned back in the direction of the fire. Surrounding his troop stood the silent forms of painted men assumed dead by those asleep at their feet.

Knives flashed across the throats of the sleeping men, loosing spurts beneath eyes that flickered with only the slightest awareness before life left them.

Firing his Colt from his waist, the gun thumped a bruise into Ellis's thigh. Its lightning burst Ritchie's head as Ellis fumbled to tuck himself away while running. A stranger dressed in Ritchie's brain matter dragged the headless body onto the embers, blotting out their light, and gave chase, his footfalls more a pounding echo of Ellis's heartbeat than Ellis's terrified jangling sprint.

Ellis whistled to his horse, but hands found him first. Fighting their grip, he tossed and kicked and fired off his pistol into a night so thick he could only see men for how they blotted out stars from view. He was dragged back toward the glow of coals on which Ritchie cooked, clothes smoldering with lines of slow crawling flame.

Someone sat among the dead. The form sang out a quavering rasp, words Ellis didn't understand, and then spoke the same, back and forth. The tune first chanted skyward then down at Ellis, who readied himself for the tear of blades. The old man then stood, walked into the dark, others followed. Ellis moved and found that no hands held him in place and no foot on his back.

"What now?" Ellis shouted. "Quit fooling! What now?"

A wolf howled, far off. Otherwise, silence answered. Not a star obscured in any which way.

Ellis whistled again.

"Rhaebus, here!"

The horse sidled up to Ellis, lips pulling at the man's shirt.

"Seems we're standing in the food dish." Ellis said, while fumbling in the dark to strip each body of valuables.

Saddlebags brimming, he mounted.

Rhaebus fled at a gallop just as the wolves fell upon the dead men; fangs ravaging the bodies with the same devouration the men had shown the frontier. The horse veered over and around obstacles Ellis couldn't see. Ellis held tight, suspecting Rhaebus might be guessing at their course. The horse soon slowed. Only then did Ellis's lungs unlock. Deep breaths filling the vast quiet between himself and the snarling feast they narrowly escaped.

Bedded down again, Ellis watched the sky sparkle in the moonless night as he listened to Rhaebus snore. Back home in Pennsylvania, nobody he'd known had ever been murdered, not by strangers nor neighbors or kin. A town of people not worth killing.

The Lord's Prayer was one of the only things Ellis had ever learned by heart, and by the time the sun came, he made plans to memorize something else for variety's sake. "*Our father,*" Ellis said to Rhaebus, "that's you and me pal. We've got the same creator. *Who art in heaven . . .* Heaven, that's green grass and fruit slop and lady horses to you. Hallowed be thy name. That's mostly tricky wording. Means His name is holy. Powerful. At least I think that's right. *By kingdom come . . .* is it 'by'? I think it is . . . *thine will be done,* so by the time of judgement, because only the Lord should be judging yours and my choices, his wishes will be carried out; *on earth as it is in heaven.* That last bit explains itself. He will make this world as it is in heaven."

He'd heard the natives committed their legends to memory. No books at all. They would tell stories to their young until the young knew them well enough to do the same when they grew older. In the firelight, the scalps slung in many strands across the saddlebags looked to Ellis like furry book jackets, disemboweled of their tales.

At sunrise Ellis's eyes felt glassy and long. Enraptured by a single spine of a barrel cactus on the farthest hill, on which a caterpillar's orange hairs swayed. If the creature were to wiggle its head or tail, Ellis might burst into a sprint. He yearned for it to move. Rhaebus snorted and nuzzled Ellis, breaking the spell.

Ellis stood, and his legs quaked like a newborn deer. He chewed some jerky, while stripping dead branches from underneath a spindly tree. Once piled, he kindled them with a dry cactus the size of his fist. He stopped often as his gut fought with its contents. Stomach pains followed and soon he doubled over twice: The first terrible. The second as if his body wanted to know if, with enough force, one could turn oneself inside out.

"That food is like a handful of blister beetles, Rhaebus."

He couldn't figure out how wine or jerky could spoil, but somehow, they had. Feeling all the weaker, Ellis rifled through his rucksack and saddlebag for every scrap of food available, piling a collection of jerky, biscuits, flasks and bottles of alcohol, water skins, apples, and a dead squirrel in a sack that Drexel must have killed and meant to eat for breakfast. It's aroma of early rot hit Ellis's nose and he was surprised to find that he enjoyed the stink.

"Seems a waste to toss this little fella seeing as he's already dead . . ."

Rhaebus turned away.

"You're right. It depends on how we cook 'em."

Ants had now claimed the jerky, biscuits, and apples, and Ellis was surprised that he found the idea of eating the ants more appealing than the food they crawled upon. He returned to the fire, added scraps of dead foliage, then began ripping the pelt from the tiny squirrel carcass, licking his fingers as black blood ran down them. His knife stripped bones of their meat with an easy practiced hand. He was disgusted at the idea of licking the rancid blood, but the tang of it was pleasant and to leave it seemed a waste. He talked with his mouth full about the best ways to prepare squirrel, and as he finished tossing aside the skin and bones, he was only holding a pulpy palm full of entrails. The meat was gone.

"Well, that was redder than most."

He snacked while watching the ants.

He reached for a cloth to wipe his hands but there was no blood left to wipe, just the slickness of his hunger.

"I guess this fire's just for sitting next to."

A hard gust of wind tossed the strands of Rhaebus's mane, the quick motion overwhelmed Ellis's attention with the promise of chase. The impulse passed, fought down like swallowed bile, but the implication remained, cold and stone, that ultimately his body would decide.

As if peeking out from behind a curtain, the crescent of a new moon flirted with the night sky. The sound of animals nearby drew Ellis to his feet, his body taut with energy. The night was young and teased him with a bouquet of sounds and smells.

Cresting a rise, Ellis smelled pollen and dander on the air and spotted a troop of familiar horses in the distance. Captain John's palomino, Lightning, and Steven and Simon's horses, a couple of buckskins named Troy and Buck. Troy after the Trojan horse of ancient lore, and Buck, because Simon had been a man of limited words and imagination from a wet town out west named something equally dull thanks to a coin flip. Maybe Simon did the same with ol' Buck. Had the coin landed otherwise, the horse might have been named something less generic, like Kelpie or Botwulf.

Sliding his way along the scree, Ellis ran lightly, but the jingle of his spurs struck him as out of place, every step disconcerting. He was reminded of his family's barn cat when a piece of nature got stuck in her fur and she had no choice but to give up on her prey and wrestle about, trying to free herself. Ellis removed the spurs from his boots and gripped one in each hand, the post and blade protruding from between his fingers.

At the base of the hill a wolf, muscles taut, was also hunting the troop. The allure of pursuit faded enough for him to realize how strange he was acting. Why would he stalk horses he could probably just holler for? And what kind of damned fool would race away from camp with no knife or gun on his person?

The wolf snuck closer to Buck, but Ellis could smell another nearby and readied himself to fight if attacked. He spotted the route of wolves winding their way toward the horses, his hands gripping the spurs tight, their many sharpened spikes forward and ready to bite.

The horses bolted and the wolves followed. The one keeping watch over Ellis loped past, leaving him feeling dismissed instead of relieved.

A stagecoach clattered into sight, drawn by its own team of horses. Again, Ellis felt naked, realizing just how foolish he was acting, now in the presence of other people. But the feeling passed quickly, and this target was all Ellis could see. The four bustling mares, the elegantly carved wheels as they spun, and surely a prize inside. In a burst, Ellis reached the road's edge and latched on as it passed, enjoying the tug that went through him as it lifted him from his feet. Within seconds he was inside.

Ellis's old dog, Argie, used to wake him at sunrise by licking his face, so he dreamed of his lost pup as he awoke to the same sensation. Opening his eyes to the carnage of at least one pronghorn antelope, a wolf licking blood from Ellis's forehead. The wolf seemed as confused as Ellis. It hurried away, looking back every few yards until it was gone.

How many men had woken to being groomed by wolves? Was this something that happened in the stories of these lands? Ellis searched the horizon, but nothing seemed familiar. His memories were muddled, like a fog that wouldn't lift. He had left Rhaebus alone. But what came after had been a whirl of impulse as hazy as a nightmare come the morning sun.

Ellis spent most of the day walking miles of looping meandering steps before he noticed Rhaebus's scent drawing him east. He eventually found the horse—heading home. He whistled like a whip crack. Rhaebus paused for an instant, then carried on into the falling darkness, faster than Ellis could walk.

Ellis jogged to catch up.

Rhaebus, ears perked, picked up his own pace.

"Dammit, boy," Ellis muttered, running to gain ground. "Rhaebus! Come on now!"

The horse trotted in a circle back toward Ellis, causing Ellis to stop with a hiss of sand at his boots. He raised his hands and inched forward.

"It's okay Rhae. Sorry to leave you alone last night."

Snorting, the horse backed up as Ellis closed the gap between them. Sweat carved streaks in the dried blood on the man's forehead.

"What's wrong, fella? What's got you spooked?"

Rhaebus was calmed by Ellis's voice, but as he came closer, the horse seemed dazed, the wild of its nature surfacing and making them strangers once more.

"You're acting like you don't recognize me at all, and . . . well, I don't get the sense I know me all that well right now either—"

Rhaebus had turned away, as if lost, and again meandered east one final time.

"Rhaebus, here!"

Ellis whistled, loud and hard. A whistle intended to call the horse from miles away. Rhaebus turned his head to the sound but kept trotting. Ellis hurried, gaining a couple of yards on the horse, sending Rhaebus galloping into the looming night.

As the waxing moon emerged, it watched a man chase a horse at a pace that grew as night fell, as if the sun, setting behind him, had been a force tugging him back, from which he was now free.

A sea of pain crashed upon Ellis the instant he awoke. A glint of light twinkled between stalactites high overhead. As his vision cleared, his body ached, and he felt a screaming in his hands, each secured to the ground, one with a pickaxe driven through the palm, the other by rope, his wrist flayed beneath its sinews. He whimpered, quaking with pain that closed his throat and held his tongue. A mining man with small wire-framed glasses perched on his nose, stared down at him.

"You are a quite the trickster, aren't you?" his captor said.

Ellis stared at his wounds. His impaled hand would never work again. "Please, my hands—" Ellis started.

"My intentions are not to help you," the man said. "You may not look like your previous self, but I assure you, this man will be made to pay for the actions of that beast."

"Please. I need a doctor," Ellis said.

"And I need a number of strong men to take the place of the ones you, the former, took it upon yourself to dismember and devour," the man said. "I need a reasonable story to tell my employer because *man-beast*, *night monster*, or even *wolf attack* won't quite do. We are equipped for wolves. We have munitions for men of all type and mammals of all shape and size, but as you have crossed the two, well, our bullets no longer seem to do the trick."

Ellis's stomach churned looking beneath the surface of his own wrist.

"Now tell me how you got this way," the man said.

"I was attacked."

His captor laughed. "Not how you are now. How you were in the night."

"I think I'm dying."

"As well you should. But you will not if I can help it. Silver runs throughout these hills. Lining them like the pockets of King Louis himself. But last night I found gold. Or it found us. A circus will pay handsomely for a monster like yourself."

"I'm just a farmer's son from Pithole, Pennsylvania."

"Oh, you're no child. Underwhelming as you seem here and now, that creature inside you has my attention."

"What did you see?" Ellis asked, worried to hear a truth as raw as his flesh.

"I saw a wolven man. A cyclone of violence. I would offer you food and water to keep you alive, but no man this side of the Mississippi has ever eaten as well as you did last night. If seeing the remains should help you come to terms with your evils, I can oblige."

Ellis shook his head. He had no recollection of what had come after sunset. Only chasing Rhaebus across a land as empty as he felt now. No hunger or thirst possessed him, but surely pain was enough to drive that from any man. He'd lost everything just to be captured by a loon who had bound him like a tent, both stake and tether.

The rattle of wagon wheels soon echoed into the cave and Ellis was manhandled and tossed into a cage with a wooden floor gouged by the claws of something great, a bear or cougar maybe.

The cart moved east, toward the nearest settlement sizable enough to rally an audience—this from snippets of conversation between the men driving. Nobody addressed Ellis directly, as he was a commodity now, they knew how to treat him as such.

Beyond the bars, the waxing moon punched through the darkening blue like a button, appearing when the world had blinked. Soon the chatter of men, alongside the clatter and toss of wagon wheels, struck Ellis as nothing more than the chirp of birds, ineffectual but charming. He no longer felt the shackles he wore as the sky called to him. The swell of evening rose within him from a tease to a tumult. The implications of the bars or the previous tenants of the cage faded as the wood beneath Ellis felt like twigs and he hungered to observe the men as they discussed their nothings of consequence. To pounce, chase, overpower, and devour.

Ellis opened his eyes to the wreckage of a trading settlement, decorated by its occupants, unmoving, and unlikely to do so. His hand no longer bandaged nor punctured. The skin folded and stretched back to good health. A crescent of scar tissue white and devoid of grain.

A silver sheriff badge had been folded in on itself and gleamed from between a dead man's broken ribs, mashed into the meat of his heart. Ellis wondered if he himself was also dead. Had been dead for days. A ghost remaining on earth more out of confusion than unwillingness to depart. Awaiting the discovery of his ragged corpse to provide some sense of certainty. Hunger had left him more than a week ago, but he had not shrunk, quite the opposite. Still, these daytime nightmares felt like he was watching the past fight the inevitable future; a violent unraveling of westward expansion. A manifest tragedy where that which his people had built on the dead was being just as brutally dismantled.

A banker lay in the street, black hat covering his face, belly emptied like a safe. Spitting image of Ellis's older brother, from what flesh remained. This bad dream, this curse, it couldn't follow him home, could it?

He picked up bits of fruit from a tavern floor, but they seemed as appetizing as pinecones. He would have kept a bottle of spirits had they not all been smashed from toppled shelves. Buzzards picked at the corpses throughout the silent township. Ellis gathered cash from the fallen. Gold nuggets, jewelry. He even packed it onto the one carriage that hadn't been destroyed or toppled. But soon found there wasn't a horse left alive to pull the damn thing.

He filled his pockets with gold and notes, slung water skins over each shoulder and, unable to shake the banker's missing entrails from his mind, he gathered food in the hope his appetite would come roaring back and prove he was normal, alive, and in as much danger as this town had been, instead of being the danger that razed it.

A man stood on a plateau overlooking the settlement with claw marks through his shirt, the fabric glued to his back with dried blood.

"You should clear out of here, sir." Ellis said. "As far as you can manage."

The man turned toward Ellis with flower petals of veiny flesh blistered across his eyes. He spoke with a broken voice. Not one hoarse with screams—but crushed by them.

"I was a fool to try to hold you."

Ellis recognized the man beneath the ravaged voice.

"I meant to profit from you after you destroyed my venture," the blind man continued, "but you are more than this world can hold. I ran while you slaughtered this town. I knew what you were, so that gave me an advantage when you revealed yourself. But I was not fast enough, only faster than the rest."

Flashes of running, the snap of bones, the pelting of bullets—slowing but never stopping him—shuddered through Ellis's mind, feeling like a daydream. Ellis ran his fingers across his chest, knots of scarring, hard just beneath the surface, like seeds of destruction. He said nothing.

"You are the wrath of God come to shuck our broken souls from this realm."

"I'm just a kid from Pithole in a land of monsters," Ellis said. "I want to go home."

"This is your home," the blind man said. "That land will always be beneath your feet."

Ellis walked east. He had come west hoping that dealing in death would build him a legacy and grant him a fortune. Now there were empty houses everywhere, wealth he could not carry, and a shadow he could not shake. No matter his offering, no witchdoctor from this land would free him, and no priest back east would believe him. If he were to chase the sunset for an eternity, could he outrun the beast inside? Or would night always find him, and anything that breathed nearby pay the cost?

Unable to concede that home could not offer some protection, he walked east, imagining Rhaebus trotting beside him, and Argie at his heels.

Within an hour he came across railroad tracks, an engine steaming, passengers boarding in fine clothes with luggage enough for a long-distance journey, and a prison car—empty. He didn't have to look far to see gallows with a substantial man hanging from them.

Ellis climbed behind the bars, pulling them closed, the latch falling into place. Looking at the thick timbers and steel that clenched around him, he hoped his cage would hold.

At noon the train chugged out of the station. Someone on the platform said that it was the Lone Liberty Crescent, next stop Emerald, Texas.

"Lord have mercy," he said to himself. But whose lord, he wondered.

The landscape grew greener as the day gave way to night. Ellis prayed that distance could break the spell. That returning home could make him whole again. He tried to picture every face he had paled, purposefully or otherwise, as he traced his evils far beyond the night of the new moon song. His apologies and promises to any god who would have him became a chant of his own, as if to never quit speaking, would leave the other unable to surface. But as the full moon swam into view over Emerald, Texas, the cart began to feel like a matchbox beneath him. As the beast emerged, his last thought was that he would join the tales written on the forgotten pages of the book covers once slung across the back of his horse. Lost.

The Clockwise People

~ Christopher Hawkins

He was looking at her hair, the way the little strands of gray caught the noonday sun to shine like ribbons of diamond, when she turned to him, smiling, and said, "Do you think that birds understand each other when they talk?"

"Birds don't talk, dear."

He scratched at his own thinning hair, the high sun hot on his scalp. "Of course they do. It's still talking, even if we don't know the words."

There were little crinkles in the upturned corners of her mouth, and her eyes were dancing. How long had it been since he had seen her eyes like that, lit from within as if every good thought had been born there? As if grief had never had a chance to touch them? "Then I suppose," he said, "they'd have to understand each other. Or else there'd be no point in talking at all."

"Well, yes. But no." She turned away from him, darkening, and just like that the moment was gone. "I mean, a goose can talk to a goose well enough. That makes perfect sense. But what if a goose is honking at a sparrow and trying to tell it something? Does the sparrow know what the goose is saying? Or is it all just a bunch of silly goose noises?"

He thought about this as their feet crunched along the gravel path. Clouds of insects swarmed in the tall grass at the shore of the little pond as starlings darted into their midst. In the distance, out past a stand of dead trees, a hawk was circling in search of a mouse.

"Well, yeah," he said, believing it more with every word. "I suppose they'd just about have to. If a fox was creeping up on their nest, they'd have to be able to warn each other, wouldn't they? It wouldn't matter if they were blackbirds, or starlings, or even seagulls. They may sound different, but they'd get the meaning all the same."

"I don't think they do," she said, shaking her head. "All those birdcalls. All that music everywhere, all those songs overlapping. If the meaning was the same it would all sound the same."

He kicked at a rock, swinging his foot out of its way to do it. "No point in music at all if it all sounds the same," he said.

"I think I'd like it better if it were all the same." Her head was turned away from him, her voice distant, as if she were talking to someone away on the other side of the pond. "I think the world would make a lot more sense that way, don't you?"

He didn't have an answer for that, certainly not one that would satisfy her, so he kept his eyes on the path ahead. They'd be leaving the pond behind soon, winding into a stand of trees and on into the wetlands beyond. The grass-hoppers would be thick there, he knew, making their bumbling leaps from cattail to sunflower and back again. It would be peaceful, the white-noise drone of their buzzings loud enough to drown away even his darkest imaginings.

"They say that birds are like guides. That they lead the souls of the dead into the next world." Her eyes were dancing again. Even beneath the shadows of the tall trees they caught the sunlight, and it made his heart lift a little. He wanted to believe what she said was true, even though he couldn't, and he knew that he could never tell her so.

"It's a lovely thought," he said.

She nodded, and said nothing more, as if she knew better than to push the point upon him. She breathed deep and inhaled the scents of the path, wildflowers and lavender, low moss and high leaves. The wind blew them against her cheeks and she turned her face against it to take their full measure.

After they had gone on a bit, he said, "I wonder if we'll see our friends again today."

"Which friends are those?"

"You know," he said. "That couple, with the little dog? Seems like every time we come out for a walk we end up seeing them sooner or later. In fact, I'm a little surprised we haven't run into them already."

"Oh, I remember now," she said, though there was something in her faraway look that made him think that she didn't. "The couple. With the little dog."

"We must be on the same schedule. Sometimes we see them in the woods, sometimes back in the park. Like they have the same route, but just walk the opposite way."

A bird fluttered down from the tall grass. It looked back at them and bounded on up the path, not taking wing but bouncing along on its little feet, putting distance between them. When it paused to look back again and saw them still coming, it hopped further away. He watched the thing, and wondered why it didn't fly.

"Oh, yes!" she said, loud enough to make him jump. "The little dog. I remember it now because it reminded me of our little Skipper. Doesn't it just remind you of Skipper, the way it's always nosing in the grass, pulling so hard on the leash that its little front paws come up off the ground?"

Birds used to be dinosaurs. He'd read that somewhere. They'd been enormous once, so big you had to crane your neck to look up at their bones in museums. Those giants were gone now. What was left pecked along in the gravel and forgot they had wings. Everything passed into something else if you let it go for long enough.

"Why are you looking at me like that?"

He'd been staring again, but in the shade of the trees her hair had lost its luster, and the lines around her eyes seemed full of dark portents.

"I dunno," he said. "Just thinking."

"You look so sad when you think."

It was talking about the leash that had done it. He could still hear the hollow tink the collar had made as it snapped free of Skipper's neck, could still see the dog's joy, the way its tongue lolled out of its mouth as it ran toward the street. He could still see Ethan rising from the grass to give chase, could still hear the naked fear in his wife's voice as she cried out for him to stop. He could hear the squeal of tires, and see the play of sunlight on the car's hood as it rocked to a stop. It had been pure chance that Ethan stumbled in the grass, that little half-step that had kept him from catching up to the little dog. Less than a second, but it had kept the boy from going under the tires. They'd sat at the curb and held him while he called out Skipper's name, but in that moment they'd barely noticed that the dog was gone.

"You blame me, don't you?" she said.

"Blame you for what?" he said.

"For all of it."

They walked together in silence for a while, the little bird hopping out in front of them, looking back at them as if it couldn't understand why they were on the path at all. At last it remembered its wings and flew away, peeping out a warning to the other birds about these two lumbering creatures that had no business in its territory. She watched it go, and kept her eyes on the space in the tall grass that it disappeared through, even after it was long out of sight.

"I couldn't have known," she said. "Not when it started. No one could have."

Little stones and bits of bark scattered at his feet, his footsteps suddenly heavy.

"You remember how it was. Nobody knew anything about it, not for sure, anyway. One week they said it was just like the flu and the next they said it wasn't. Then they said you didn't need masks, until they said you did, and even then it got all political and everyone was shouting over each other until you just wanted to put your hands over your ears, there was so much of it."

He listened to the distant peeping of the birds, their sounds measured and mechanical, like the beeping of hospital machines. He listened to the sounds of their footsteps, shushing softly, like the hiss of a respirator.

"But I did everything right," she said, "or at least I did everything that I knew how to do right. I cleaned all the time. I made him wash his hands. I was careful. I tried to make sure he was careful, too, but it just . . ."

The wind through the trees like the pulling of a hospital curtain. The drone of cicadas like a flatlined EKG.

"None of it mattered. Not one thing." She stopped walking and he turned back to look at her. The sun in his eyes made him squint.

"I did everything I knew how to do and it happened anyway. Sometimes bad things just happen like that. It doesn't make it my fault."

"Maybe," he said.

She folded her arms. With the sun at her back filtering through the trees, the glow was back in her hair. She seemed lit from within, all grief and fire and rage, and seeing her like that broke his heart.

"Maybe? What do you mean, maybe?"

"I mean," he said, "that maybe there was something you could have done, something I could have done, if we had just known what it was."

"No . . ."

"I mean, what if there was some choice we made, some minor little thing that we did without realizing, and if we hadn't made that choice—that thoughtless, insignificant choice—then it never would have happened the way it did."

"Stop."

"Like, what if there was a way that he'd never gotten sick at all? If I'd just taken a little longer eating breakfast one day, or made him go back upstairs to change his shirt when he was wearing long sleeves like he always did, even when it was too hot outside. Or if we'd taken the other way around on our walk one day, or if he'd sat in a different seat on the school bus."

"Stop it," she said. "I don't want to hear this."

"Or if I'd run that yellow light on the way to the hospital and we'd gotten him there two minutes sooner. It's like the day Skipper got hit by that car. If the boy hadn't tripped, the car would have hit him too. But what made him trip? Were his pants too long? Were his shoes tied too tight? Were they not tight enough?"

"I said stop it!"

"Or was it just a low spot in the ground? Like maybe someone was playing football and fell down on that exact spot and made a little divot there, not so much as you'd notice, but just enough to make it so the boy would fall down right there, a week, maybe even a month or a year later. Just one little change like that, just one, and he'd still be here, walking right down this path with us, right now."

"Stop saying it! You can't think things like that. You just can't!" She was doubled over now, her hands pressed against her ears as if she could will his words away. But he'd said them, now, after thinking them a thousand times, and there was no taking them back. He wanted to go to her, to take her in his arms and hold her close, even if it meant that she would only pound her fists against his chest and shove him away. He'd done nothing wrong, and yet he knew that it was no less than he deserved.

"I just miss him, is all," he said at last.

She raised her head to him. Her eyes were dry and there was a hardness in them now that he'd only seen there once before. It was as if a bright light had gone out of the world, and he feared it would never return.

"You can't say things like that," she said. "When you say things like that it's like he's dying all over again."

"I know."

"You can't say things like that."

"I know."

They continued up the path, out of the wetlands and toward the darkening shade of the trees. She kept a half step behind him, as if she was not quite ready to walk by his side. He kept his eyes on the path ahead, on the distant point where it curved, disappearing among the trees.

"I think you're right about the birds," he said.

"About the way they talk?"

He shook his head. "About the souls of the dead. It makes me feel like he's safe. Like there's this whole other world where he's not gone, but just . . . waiting."

She wrapped her arm around his and squeezed reassuringly. He felt his mood lift a little, and resolved to say nothing more about it, to finish their walk in silence if that's what it took not to upset her again. He wished that he could stop thinking about it too, but his mind would not lay still. It coiled like a snake, twisting in on itself until he no longer knew where one thought began and the other ended.

In the end, it was her mouth, not his, that gave them voice.

"I wonder if there really is another world," she said, tightening around his arm, pulling him close. "If there are then maybe he's happy now, wherever he went off to. Maybe it's even the same place that Skipper went to, and the two of them are playing together right now."

He said nothing. He just stared out at the curve in the path, hoping that would be the end of it, that some new thought would come along to distract her. But her grip on him was getting tighter, and he knew then that she would not let it go.

"And what if there's more than one? I mean, isn't that what the scientists say? That every choice makes a whole new universe? A whole new reality branching off from the old one every time someone makes even the smallest choice?"

Above their heads, a blackbird lighted on a branch, bending it beneath its weight. A refugee from the asteroid. One more survivor of extinction.

"Or the smallest mistake."

This last she said softly, almost at a whisper. He craned his neck upward, watching the bird, hoping that she would notice the motion and begin to watch it too, that it would distract her from these thoughts, this folly, that they could finish their walk and say no more of it.

"Because if," she said. "If all those other worlds are out there, then there would have to be one where he never died at all. Maybe more than one."

"You're right," he said. "We shouldn't think about such things."

"How many of those worlds do you think there are? Dozens? Hundreds? Where you ran that red light? Where he took another seat on the bus? Where we went around the path the opposite way?"

No, he thought. *Don't do this.*

"Maybe there are more worlds where he didn't die than there are where he did. Maybe all those worlds are the *right* worlds, and living is exactly what he was supposed to do? What if all the worlds where he died are the wrong worlds, and they were never supposed to have been made in the first place?"

He felt her grip tighten and knew that she had arrived at the same place he had, that those darkest thoughts that he had failed to keep hidden had finally infected her own. He felt the press of her nails against his skin and wished in that moment that he could pull away.

She inhaled sharply, barely daring to speak. "What if this is the only one?"

Around them, insects buzzed as birds hopped and chirped in the treetops. A sharp pop sounded near the ground, some small creature in the underbrush. Still he kept his eyes on the path, on that distant bend that was straightening now, threatening to reveal more of the way ahead.

"We should have seen them by now," he said.

"Who?"

"Those others," he said. "The ones who always end up walking towards us."

"Oh, the ones with the little dog."

He nodded. "I thought we would have seen them by now."

She stopped then, holding onto his arm so tightly that he had no choice but to stop with her. Together they stood, still as statues, listening to the sounds of the forest ahead, of the reedy pond behind.

"We should go back," she said.

The air around them was still, but in the treetops it blew hard and set the branches clacking against each other.

"We're fine," he said, and as it left his mouth it sounded almost like a question.

She shook her head. "Something's not right. Can you feel it? I know you can feel it."

He *could* feel it. He felt it down to his bones, but all it did was make him that much more anxious to move on, to see what lay around the bend in the path. "It'll take longer to get home than if we keep going forward."

"I don't care," she said. "I want to go back."

"Nonsense," he said. "All that talk has got you spooked, is all. You'll feel better once we're out of these trees."

"I'll feel better when we turn around." Her nails in his

arms were talons now, about to draw blood. "Why can't we just turn around?"

Her eyes were wide now, shining. He wanted to do as she asked, but could not. He tried to make his legs move to turn around, but they wouldn't budge.

"I see the way you keep looking up the path," she said. "You're looking for them, aren't you?"

"Looking for who?"

"Those people! The ones with the little dog."

Once more he searched ahead into the distance. The path was empty, the air silent, and from somewhere deep within himself he felt a sharp pang of despair.

"You're so anxious to see them again, but do you even remember what they look like?" She let go of his arm, folded her own across her chest. "Go on. Describe them to me. Describe them and I'll keep walking down this path. I won't turn around. I won't even look back. Just describe them to me."

He opened his mouth to speak but no words came out. There was nothing in his thoughts to form them. No memory. Just a blank space. Empty silhouettes against a field of brown and green.

"How old are they? Is her hair long or short? Is he handsome? Ugly? Do you remember anything about them? Anything at all?"

"Well, the dog is small, like Skipper," he said at last, though he was no longer sure of even that. The wind reached down from the treetops and sent a scatter of dead leaves across the path. All of a sudden, turning back felt like a good idea, the right idea, if only he could will his body to do it.

"I don't remember them either," she said softly. "I know they were there. We must have passed them a dozen times, maybe even a hundred, but I can't picture their faces. After all those times I should be able to picture their faces."

"They . . ." The words were slow to come, his mind stuck in molasses. "They had a kid with them." Again the words came out like a question, but as he strained to picture those walking silhouettes he could just about make out a small child walking with them, walking hand in hand. Was it true? Or was it just his own wishful thinking?

"Why can't I picture their faces?"

She stared at him, her mouth trembling, her eyes pleading. Had there been a child with them? Had he remembered that right? And if they were to meet again, would the man be balding like he was? The same height? The same weight? And would the woman be walking quickly with the sun shining in her eyes as the little dog pulled her along by his leash? What then? What would they do if these people passed right by them, close enough to touch?

"You're right," he said. "We have to go back."

He tugged at her arm, but she would not turn around. Her head was turned and she would not look at him. She stared up the path, and inhaled with a gasp.

"There they are!"

He followed her gaze to the distant bend in the path. They were moving there between the trees, too far away to make out their features. Two figures, walking unhurried, taking their time as if time were never a concern. The little dog led them, rebellious and wild at the end of its leash.

"Come on now," he said. His mouth was dry and his voice was barely a whisper. "We have to go."

She pulled free of his grip, tugging away so fiercely that it was as if his touch had burned her. "I have to see," she said. Already she was moving away from him, leaving him behind. On the path ahead, the woman turned to the man and the woman must have been smiling from the way she threw her head back, from the way she slipped her arm around the man's bicep. Their faces were shaded by the trees and they were walking together so closely that he could almost imagine another silhouette trailing behind them, smaller, hurrying to keep up, though he could not tell for sure.

"Please!" He was shouting now, and he could hear the tears building in his voice, threatening to ruin him. "I'm sorry. Let's go back. We can still go back."

He set off at a run to follow her, but knew that she was already too far away.

CONTRIBUTORS

Daniel Dagris

Daniel Dagris is a Pacific Northwest author of rural fantasy and horror, with a literary bent. His work has been nominated for the Pushcart Prize, received honorable mention from *Glimmer Train*, and has appeared in *Orca Literary Journal, Open Ceilings*, and elsewhere.

Phillip E. Dixon

Phillip E. Dixon is an English Professor from Las Vegas whose fiction has appeared in *Cosmic Horror Monthly, The Fabulist, Book of Matches Literary Magazine*, and elsewhere. He holds an MFA in Writing from Lindenwood University, speaks lousy German to his two cats, and spends his rent money on coffee as a good addict should.

J. V. Gachs

J.V. Gachs is a Spanish classicist, and writer, currently working as a Latin teacher. Writing in English and Spanish her work has been featured in anthologies like Scott J. Moses' *What One Wouldn't Do* and Chelsea Pumpkins' *AHH! That's What I Call Horror!* Her debut novel, *Epiphany,* will be released by Off Limits Press in December 2023. Obsessed with sudden death, ghosts, and female villains, she always writes with a cat (or two) in her lap.

Find more of her work: jvgachs.com

J. Anthony Hartley

J. Anthony Hartley is an Australian/British author and poet. He has had pieces appear in *Short Fiction, Hybrid Fiction, Short Circuit, The Periodical, Abandon Journal,* among others and has had poetry in T*he Quarter(ly), New Myths, Space & Time* and in *Twenty Two Twenty Eight.*

He currently resides in Germany and can be found at http://www.iamnotaspider.com. He no longer lives on Twitter or whatever it might be called.

Christopher Hawkins

Christopher Hawkins is an award-winning horror writer, and the author of the short story collection *Suburban Monsters.* His debut novel, *Downpour,* arrives in October. He is the former editor of the *One Buck Horror* anthology series and co-chair of the Chicagoland chapter of the Horror Writers Association. When he's not writing, he spends his time exploring old cemeteries, lurking in museums, and searching for a decent cup of tea.

For more information about his upcoming projects, visit his website, www.christopher-hawkins.com, or follow him on Twitter @chrishawkins and Instagram at @hawkinswrites.

John Klima

John Klima previously worked in New York's publishing jungle before returning to school to earn his Master's in Library Science. He now works full time as the Technology Manager of a large public library. John edited and published the Hugo Award-winning genre zine *Electric Velocipede* from 2001 to 2013.

When he is not conquering the world of indexing, John writes short stories and novels. He and his family live in the Midwest.

Reggie Kwok

Reggie Kwok dreams of dragons in his sleep when he is not summoning their powers for writing. He holds a B.A. in English and a master's in education. He currently lives in Massachusetts, USA. He had a short story published at *Samjoko Magazine* and another one forthcoming at *Zooscape*.

His Twitter is @KwokReggie.

Jon Lasser

Jon Lasser lives in Seattle, WA with his wife and two children. His stories have appeared in *Lightspeed, Interzone, Galaxy's Edge,* and elsewhere. He's a graduate of the Clarion West writers workshop.

Find him online at twoideas.org.

Gerri Leen

Gerri Leen lives in Northern Virginia and originally hails from Seattle. In addition to being an avid reader, she's passionate about horse racing, tea, and collecting encaustic art and raku pottery. She has work appearing or accepted by *The Magazine of Fantasy and Science Fiction*, *Nature, Strange Horizons, Daily Science Fiction,* and others. She's edited several anthologies for independent presses, is finishing some longer projects, and is a member of SFWA and HWA.

See more at gerrileen.com.

Mark Mills

A Cincinnati resident, Mark Mills teaches composition, literature, film, philosophy, music appreciation, and basic Noa robotic. He has published work in *Tor.com, Grievous Angel, Necrotic Tissue, Short Story America*, and other publications. He worked on and appeared in several low budget films, including *Satanic Yuppies, Live Nude Shakespeare, Chickboxin' Underground, Zombie Cult Massacre*, and *Uberzombiefrau*. Having recently survived advanced stage cancer, he hopes to have his brain implanted in a robotic body and avoid any further health woes.

PAMELA COLMAN SMITH

The tarot images in this issue of Arcana are from the deck illustrated by Pamela Colman Smith. It was released in 1909 as the Rider-Waite deck (so named, at that time, in reference to its publisher, William Rider & Son). It remains the most influential and widely used tarot deck. While the impetus for the deck came from Arthur Edward Waite, Colman Smith was responsible for the iconography of the cards.

Pamela Colman Smith also illustrated over twenty books, wrote two collections of Jamaican folklore, edited two magazines, and ran the Green Sheaf Press, a small press devoted to women writers. She continued to write and illustrate throughout her life.

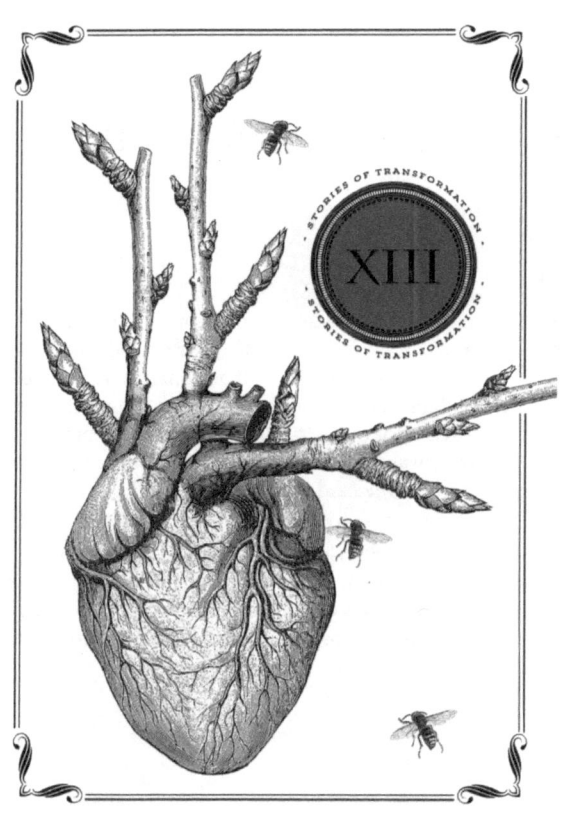

STORIES OF TRANSFORMATION

XIII

STORIES OF TRANSFORMATION

XIII

The thirteenth Tarot card is Death, and he is a symbol not of the end, but of transformation and rebirth. This is the genesis and root of *Thirteen: Stories of Transformation*. The twenty-eight authors of this collection are voices—new and old—who are not afraid to explore what comes next. Whether it be a life after death, a life without love, a life filled with hunger, or the life shared by a ghost. These are stories of the weird, the mythic, the fantastic, the futuristic, the supernatural, and the horrific.

With stories by Liz Argall • M. David Blake • Richard Bowes • George Cotronis • Amanda C. Davis • Julie C. Day • Jetse de Vries • Jennifer Giesbrecht • Daryl Gregory • Rik Hoskin • Rebecca Kuder • Claude Lalumière • Marc Levinthal • Grá Linnaea • Alex Dally MacFarlane • Juli Mallett • Lyn McConchie • Fiona Moore • Gregory L. Norris • Adrienne J. Odasso • Cat Rambo • Andrew Penn Romine • David Tallerman • Tais Teng Richard Thomas • Fran Wilde • A. C. Wise • Christie Yant

Edited by Mark Teppo.

Available at independent bookstores everywhere.

http://www.underlandpress.com

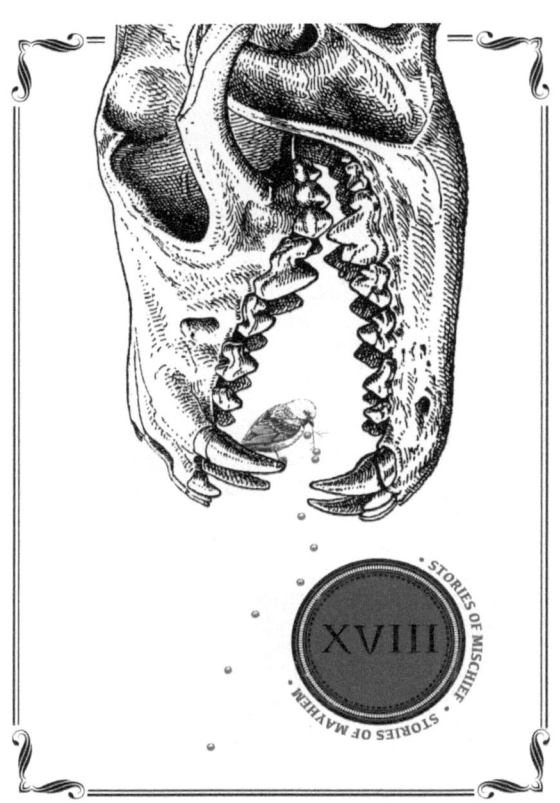

XVIII

STORIES OF MISCHIEF · STORIES OF MAYHEM

XVIII

The eighteenth Tarot card is the Moon, and those who raise their arms to her know she offers Mercy and Severity in equal measure. This is the great river at night, where wolves howl and all doors are open. All futures are possible, and every truth is elusive. This is the source and passion of *Eighteen: Stories of Mischief & Mayhem.* These twenty-four stories from voices—old and new—celebrate the inevitability of fate, the horror of prophecy, and the shivering delight of not knowing what comes next.

Cross over the threshold with us, and explore the strange, the weird, and the fantastic. Do not fear what lies ahead. It is the same as what came before. The only difference is you. This is *Eighteen*, and nothing will be the same.

With stories by Forrest Aguirre • Darin Bradley • Christopher East • Scott Edelman • Nicole Feldringer • Ben Gamblin • Ingrid Garcia • A. P. Howell • Emma Johnson-Rivard • E. E. King • Jessie Kwak • Shannon Lawrence • Gerri Leen • Mark Mills • Christi Nogle Tammie Painter • Josh Rountree • Erica Sage • Lorraine Schein • J. Dee Stanley • Richard Thomas • John Waterfall • Wendy N. Wagner • Todd Zack

Edited by Mark Teppo.

Available at independent bookstores everywhere.

http://www.underlandpress.com

www.ingramcontent.com/pod-product-compliance
Lightning Source LLC
Chambersburg PA
CBHW050405110726
47899CB00008B/2658